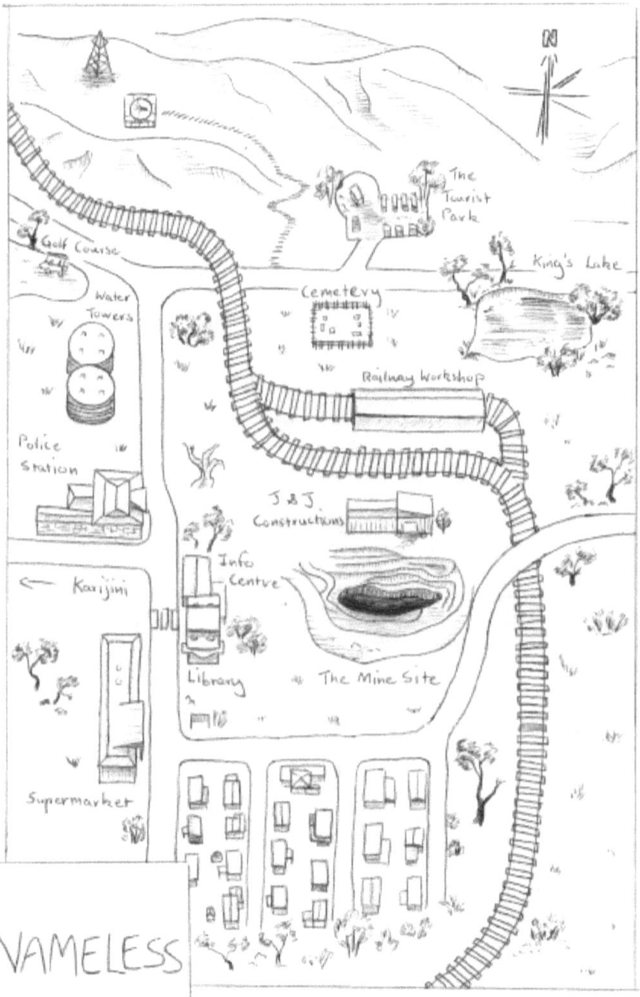
N
The Tourist Park
King's Lake
Golf Course
Cemetery
Water Towers
Railway Workshop
Police Station
J & J Constructions
Info Centre
Karijini
Library
The Mine Site
Supermarket

NAMELESS

Nameless

Mel Hammond

Published by Mel Hammond, 2025.

NAMELESS

First edition. June 28, 2025.

Copyright © 2025 Mel Hammond.

ISBN: 978-1763744479

Written by Mel Hammond.

Table of Contents

This one's for you, Shirl. For your ever patient tour-guiding around Australia. No matter where I find myself, you've been there first and can tell me where to park my rig.

Nameless

A TOWN IN THE MIDDLE of nowhere
    with a reputation built on forgetting why you're there in the first place
    A Rio town bought and paid for in another century,
    a place where deals are done, and hands are shaken in the far-off city
of Perth.
    Where blokes cram close in company-issue dongas
    to earn their lot and get the fuck out
    before their missus runs off with a suit while their backs are turned.
    Nameless, where bad things happen to good people
    and there is no such thing as karma.
    An unmarked grave, a hand-carved cross, an unclaimed fortune.
    A moonless night during a summer storm
    An accident on the mountain, a witness nobody suspects.
    Things begin to unravel when a woman arrives in town
    to claim what's rightfully hers.

Prologue - 1993

WHERE DO STORIES BEGIN, Rosie wonders. She has always liked stories—with her as the heroine of course.

She sits, arms wrapped around her knees, and stares into the night, mesmerised by the flickering lights down in the valley.

A moth to a lamp.

Suddenly, she stands and twirls her skirts. *Freedom*. She tests the word with a moue of her lips and spreads her arms wide. Accidentally, she tilts her head too far back and stumbles a little, laughing up to the night sky as she regains her balance.

The kaleidoscope of stars laughs back at the woman who is crazy-mad to dance so close to the edge of the mountain, with nothing but air to break her fall.

"Dance with me." She reaches down and pulls her friends to their feet.

Together they twirl, their skirts a rainbow of colours billowing around them. There is no wind but that's okay. They create their own as they jitterbug and do the swim and rock around the clock.

They giggle as only new best friends can as they stumble on the rocky ground and hold out steadying hands to each other. Rosie marvels at her new friends, the coiffure-haired woman with her complicated braids and bobby pins, and the quiet woman beside her with her shell-framed glasses and neatly buttoned shirt tucked into her skirt.

Rosie, who is tall and dark and exotic with loose hair and languid movements, twirls her glitter-crocheted shawl around her head while her new friends try to emulate her but instead tangle themselves in ungainly limbs and fall down laughing.

She tosses the shawl into the night and watches it flutter effortless into the valley below.

The feeling is heady.

And so is the drug of a starlit night under an outback sky while their men are busy with their important meeting somewhere in the lights of the valley below. On the mountain, the women celebrate their freedom: to laugh and drink green vermouth with lemonade, and to dance and twirl and sing.

Rosie claps her heels together, Mexican-style, as her red skirt billows around her and her hair spins free of its gold daisy-chain headband. She laughs and throws herself backwards onto the hard earth and makes a snow angel in the red dirt with her bare feet moving out and in and out and in, while her arms above her head make the same movements.

Her new friends place their vermouths to one side and join her.

Angels in the moonlight.

Rosie extends her hands to them. "Let's count the stars," she says.

Trusting fingers entwine with hers. "I am such a bad influence, aren't I?"

Her new friends laugh. "You are an influence, that's for sure," the coiffured one says. "But one we need around here."

Rosie stills. "Is it really that bad?"

"Look around you. Our men do deals while we cook their meals and wash their clothes and iron neat creases into the shoulders of their shirts."

"Well, we're here now." Rosie jumps to her feet. She stretches down her hands and pulls her friends up with her, and together they jump out of the angel shapes they have made.

"Wicked," Rosie says. "We're angels in the dust."

She walks over to the edge of the outcrop and looks out. In this moment, in this place, she is heroine of a story she has been writing forever.

She feels a tug at her skirt as the button-down one pulls her back from the edge. "More drink, please. I think I like it."

Rosie smiles. She has made her new friends, who are already heady from dancing on a mountain in the dark, drunk. On green vermouth and a little something extra.

She makes more drinks, stirs them with her finger—the white powder dissolving like it's never been—and passes them to her friends. "Have you ever wondered if you can fly?"

The coiffured woman snorts. "If I could fly, I'd be out of this fucking dog-hole for sure." She seems shocked at the admission and Rosie wonders if she knows she has said the F word aloud. She wonders what it would take to get her to say that other word, the word men sling around in pubs like an insult, *don't waste your time on her mate she's a tight arsed cunt,* while they hope they'll get lucky anyway.

Rosie learned long ago a woman's power is centred in her cunt. Hold out long enough and you hit the happily-ever-after jackpot.

"Do you think they're wondering what we're up to tonight, our husbands?" the button-down one asks.

"Not on your life.' The coiffured one sips her drink and grimaces. "All they're interested in is the occasional fuck and a feed on the table at night."

Rosie drops between her new friends and slings an arm over each of their shoulders. "So young to be so cynical. Shall we get naked?"

The women stiffen.

Rosie realises she has gone too far. She urges more drink, and they sip, the moment forgotten.

"How are we going to get home?" the button-down one asks eventually. "We came to watch the sunset. And now it's too dark to climb back down."

"This is our kingdom." Rosie throws her arms out expansively. "Why would we want to leave?"

The coiffured-haired one's hand is still on her vermouth. "Because if we're not home in the morning our blokes will kill us. And if word gets out what we're doing up here there'll be hell to pay."

Rosie eyes her curiously. "Have you ever done anything you wanted to do, you know, just for you?"

"For me?" The woman cocks her head. "No one has ever asked me that."

Rosie drops her head onto her shoulder. "You know what I want?" she says. "I want to fly off this mountain to the other side of the desert where the sea is gentle, the sand is white and a rainforest with soft ferns drips cool water onto our dusty lips."

She knows she is being poetic, but it is a night for poetry as the hum of her blood courses through her veins. She closes her eyes and lets the feeling carry her over the red hills and across the desert to the other side of the country where women wear pearls over Mohair twinsets and dine in a city with harbour views and an opera house.

She is a heroine on the stage—she feels the spotlight on her face. She smiles. The audience applauds and she takes a bow.

She hands her drink to her new friends. "Watch me."

She rises from the dirt between them. And stands, listening to the silence. The crowd erupts as she holds out her skirts and takes a curtsy, deep and low. She hears the cheers as they begin to throw bunches of flowers—Damascus Roses—at her feet.

She gathers them in her arms. Makes kissing shapes with her mouth and flings the kisses to her audience with dramatic hands. "Thank you, thank you."

The spotlight is starting to overheat, and she feels her make-up drip, but still she stands and still the crowd cheers.

After the applause, she drops the roses into her friends' open laps and walks towards her audience.

They cheer as she launches herself into their waiting arms.

She falls slowly forward, heroine in her own story.

The Present

Chapter 1

IT'S forty-five degrees and she's sweating a bitch.

"Wait here, Trouble." She loops the dog's leash around an outdoor table leg and gives him a quick scratch. Blessed aircon smacks her in the face as she enters the bakery.

"Coffee to go, luv?"

It's like she's been here forever, not just pulled into the local Tourist Park and flipped open the roof-top of her van.

"Thanks, Ray," she says.

The baker passes her a scalding two-heaped-teaspoons no-brand coffee in a Styrofoam cup. *Start a fuckin' four-by with the shit*, they tell her back at the Tourist Park. *Ain't nothin' better this side of the Hammersley.*

Coffee in hand, she unties her dog, and they set off down the concourse, past a café named *Karijini*, a chemist with pretty things displayed in the windows and a brand-name supermarket alongside a regulation bottle shop where a licence is needed to procure alcohol. Trouble growls at a sculpted kangaroo that stands two heads taller than her, and she gives him a quick pat for protecting her from the steel-clawed beast.

They cross the street at the crosswalk, giving way to a mine vehicle, its fluoro insignia covered in red dirt. It's too hot yet for tourists, and woman and dog are glad to rest in the shade of the hot pink bougainvillea, beside a dirt-orange *Welcome to Ashburton* sign with its big I for Information.

Karin gazes at the Information Centre, with its Karijini Gorge tours and souvenirs boasting deep russet-coloured escarpments, highlighting the ore the Pilbara is famous for.

She settles for a visit to the library. "Sorry, mate," she says, tying Trouble's leash to a bench leg. "You need to wait outside. I won't be long."

"Bring him in," the library assistant, Tammy says with a smile. "It's too bloody hot out there for the poor mongrel."

Karin smiles and unties the dog, who shoots a droopy-eyed *thank you* at the library assistant and drools his appreciation onto the white tiles at her feet.

"Cute." Tammy offers her hand for a lick. "He can stay here with me while you wander if you like."

"Thanks."

"We get forty new books every month. Let me know if we haven't got what you want, and we can get it in for you."

Karin hesitates. "Thanks, but I'm just in town for my friend's wedding."

"Jess Maskell's? Everyone's been talking about it. Wedding of the century around these parts."

"I thought I might see if I can find some pictures from when we were growing up. Do you have any old local gazettes, school year books or anything?"

Tammy frowns. She is twenty if she is a day, and anything prior to the last couple years is beyond her living memory. "We have a local history section," she says. "But most of what you'd be looking for will be in the old Pilbara newspapers."

"You have old newspapers?" Karin tries to keep the interest from her voice.

"Sure," Tammy says. "Going back to the seventies. We're in the process of scanning and uploading them onto our Library Management System. I can show you where we're up to if you like."

"That would be great," Karin says. "Is there anywhere private I can look at them?"

"Sure. Let me get permission from my boss. You'll probably have to join the library. Then you can come out the back and use my computer. Bring the dog."

Karin nods and goes to browse the Local History section while Tammy sets up.

She wanders past the Fiction section, noting crime writers. Chris Hammer, Christian White and Gary Disher adorn the shelves alongside popular women's fiction by the likes of Rachel Johns and Tricia Stringer. There's some horror and sci-fi, but clearly crime and romance win the day in the outback.

She keeps walking and squats down in front of a single shelf labelled Local History. There is a photographic book of the Pilbara with stunning images, alongside a few local mining histories and several new-looking books about the First Nations people of the Hammersley.

She pulls a mining history off the shelf that notes the irony of the name Mt Nameless, where iron ore man, Lang Hancock, claims discovery of the second highest mountain in Western Australia but fails to give it a name.

She tucks the book under her arm and heads back to the desk, where Tammy tells her she needs to join the library to be able to access the newspapers.

"Come with me," she says, after she hands Karin a laminated Shire of Ashburton library card. "We'll get you settled. I can print out any pictures you want for the wedding if you save them to a file."

With Trouble settled at her feet, Karin waits until Tammy is busy serving other customers before turning her attention to the computer and searching for the Hammersley News. She scans the dates until she reaches the year she wants.

Soon she is lost in the headlines of June 2009, a narrative of the town framed in terms of tonnes of iron ore and market prices, what the

Pilbara is known for, and the people making billions selling it to the highest bidder. There's mention of new technologies at a shareholder meeting but the article is general in nature and the words *cutting edge* are liberally sprinkled throughout.

Karin snaps a couple of photos on her phone and continues to scan. *The Death of a Railway Man*. It is what she has been looking for but now it is in front of her she finds she can't look past the headline and the picture that accompanies it.

She stares at her father's face.

Our father, who art in heaven.

Who threw her in air and caught her when she came giggling down.

Hallowed be thy name. Who brushed her hair and tied rough ribbons and kissed her off to school.

Thy kingdom come. Who promised his princess she could be anything she wanted to be when she grew up.

Now and forever. Whose happily-ever-after promises stopped when she was sixteen and old enough to know he had been lying to her all along.

Amen.

She emails the article to herself. *A Tribute to a Mining Legend.* She'll read it later when she is alone.

Trouble nudges her knee.

She scratches his head. "Time to go, hey mate."

Karin closes the computer, hooks the dog on his leash, and returns to the desk to check out the book. *Rio and the Pilbara: A Mining History.*

Tammy looks at her curiously. "You interested in the mine? There's a mine tour you might enjoy. I've heard it's really good."

Karin smiles vaguely as she exits. She knows all she needs to about the mine, and her father's job driving the trains that pull 250 wagons of ore 800 kilometres through the winding hills of the Pilbara to the sea.

What she doesn't know is the details of his death or the reason for it. *A Tribute to a Mining Legend* may not give her the closure she craves, but it will hopefully give her a place to start.

Because one thing is for certain: she's not leaving without solving the mystery surrounding her father's death and holding those accountable who saw fit to leave her father for dead on a lonely railway siding in the dark of night all those years ago.

Karin does not believe in karma.

Nor does she believe those who killed her father got their just desserts.

She believes in facts.

And the facts show that thirty million dollars was deposited into her mother's savings account after her father's death.

"Follow the money," she murmurs to the dog as hot air blasts them outside the library. "The answer always lies with the money."

Chapter 2

THEY walk down Central Road, past the Anzac memorial, to the High School. Karin smiles at the memory of a teacher who couldn't remember her name in English class, while Trouble sniffs at a dead corella struck by a car and squashed into the bitumen like a tattoo.

"No hope for him, sorry, mate. Beak and feather disease. Not a good way to go."

They follow the road till it ends and turn left across an open paddock towards the railway line. The line's journey through the town is secured by six-foot wire-mesh fencing. There are two tracks that appear from a long sweeping curve on the right, and a single track from the left. The tracks converge and disappear through a concrete overpass that frames Mt Nameless in the distance. There is a footpath beside a road across the overpass that provides a safe traverse from one side to the railway tracks to the other.

Karin climbs up onto the road and stands on the overpass, Trouble at her side. Ahead, the railway tracks are arrow-straight until a junction where the tracks split, one curving left at the foot of the mountain and one continuing its journey into distant hills.

On her left are railway office dongas, coupled with the detritus of mining equipment needed to support a 24/7 autonomous railway. Sodexo, the company charged with supplying staff and crew for the mining operation, is on one corner with its No Entry Without Authorisation signs. On another corner begins a variety of truck hires, an auto-repairer, a straggle of Go West tour buses, and a Pilbara Food Services warehouse. At the end of the cul-de-sac, with an unobstructed view of the mountain, is J&J Construction, the engineering company run by Jess and her father.

Karin turns her attention to the tracks below her, imagining a train lumbering through on its way to the coast with its wagons of ore. Braking at a red light, slowing, as only a two hundred and fifty wagon train can, a kilometre down the track at the foot of the mountain.

Karin closes her eyes. Recalls the words from the article she found in the library. The body of James Baxter found underneath the wheels of a train. Like it is an accident. Karin's fist tightens on the dog's leash.

Trouble leans against her like he senses her distress. She loosens her grip and gives him an apologetic scratch, but her eyes are wet and her vision is blurred.

"How long does an ore train take to pass, Trouble? Two hundred and fifty wagons at seventy-five kilometres an hour... Two minutes? Five?"

Surely someone would have noticed the ore-hauling beast grinding to a halt in the night. Or at least noted the absence of the usual roar of its passing. An obstacle on the track would fire off the emergency brakes and set off a signal. The mine would send someone out to investigate.

"What are we missing, Trouble?"

The dog sits patiently at her feet, as if he knows his mistress is doing important work and that they will not leave this place until she is ready.

She frowns.

The article this morning had referred to her father's contribution to the introduction of automated trains to the Pilbara. At least in the early stages. Before his untimely demise. A man of vision who did not live to see his ideas come to fruition.

"That's it." She swipes a hand across her eyes, and her gaze narrows in on the point where the track curves towards the mountain. "The trains weren't automated back then, Trouble. Someone would have had to manually stop the train. The train would have had a driver in charge of the emergency braking system."

A driver who would have had to file a report. Someone who knew what happened that night. All Karin has to do is find out who it was and ask them. *How did my father end up dead under the wheels of one of his own fucking trains?*

Yeah, sure. Like they will tell her after all this time. Don't worry your pretty little head about it, they will say. And they will smile like they are protecting her from a gruesome truth. Like they did when she was sixteen. Only she is no longer sixteen. And she refuses to be treated like someone who needs protecting. Her pretty little head contains a laser-sharp brain honed by the rigours of old school investigative journalism. The days are long gone that her pretty little head is not up for the job. She sees their platitudes with the clarity of a journalist with two Walkleys to her name. And she will not be swayed by their condescension.

She turns away from the railway tracks and follows the path off the overpass, Trouble pressed close at her side.

She looks down. Trouble's tongue is hanging out. She shouldn't have walked this far in the heat, she knows, and Trouble is thirsty. In front of her is the mine site with its No Entry sign in bold capital letters. She glances around and comes to a decision. It is not her fault that she is ignoring the No Entry sign. She is doing it for her dog.

She pushes open the chain-mesh gates, which are bolted, but unlocked. She strides towards the railway donga as if she has a right to be there.

The mine's office receptionist stares up at her, startled, as she pushes open the door.

"Water," Karin explains. "For the dog."

Trouble knows he has a role to play. He sits back on his haunches and stares at the receptionist, his tongue hanging out, saliva dripping in a puddle onto the tiled floors.

"Outside," the receptionist starts, then closes her mouth firmly. One look at Karin and the receptionist knows she isn't going to get anywhere with her demand. "I'll get a bowl," she says, tightlipped.

Karin nods, but her gaze has moved beyond the receptionist to the wall behind her. A picture of a mining crew in front of a train. She steps around the reception desk for a closer look.

She stands, her arms crossed, and stares at the picture, scanning the faces till she finds the one she is looking for. She'd recognise those eyes anywhere, even in black and white.

The train is an old AR 63. Her father is sporting a train driver's hat, worn backwards, a cocky grin on his face. He is in his element, leaning into the photo, his gaze confident. His mates jostle either side of him, oozing blokey camaraderie—but it is her father who owns the photo. A man among men. Confident of his own worth. The same worth that dominates their loungeroom mantelpiece back home in the city. Except there, he isn't surrounded by his mates.

She leans into the photograph and stares at her father's image. Blistered eyes juxtaposed onto a handsome face. When had she stopped loving him and started doubting? Followed by several years of angry crying. Until finally, all that is left is an empty feeling in her heart where her hero Daddy had once resided.

The receptionist returns and Karin swings around. "When did the trains become automated?"

The receptionist frowns. "Before my time," she says shortly. She has no intention of thawing to the deranged girl or her equally deranged dog. She holds out the bowl. Karin takes the hint. She moves away from the reception desk to the water cooler near the door and helps herself to a plastic cup of icy cold water. And another one. When she finishes draining the second cup, she turns back to the receptionist.

She softens her smile. "Apologies for barging in," she says. "But we walked into town from the Tourist Park not realising it would get hot so quickly." She offers a shrug that says *hapless tourist*, but neither she nor the receptionist are fooled.

The receptionist nods. "The heat out this way is a killer."

Karin wonders if there is a slight emphasis on the word *killer*. She thinks she has been discreet with her enquiries. But it is clear the receptionist has heard things, and she is wary.

"My Dad used to work for the mine," Karin says. "He drove trains back in the day." She nods at the wall behind the receptionist's head. "Mind if I take another look at the photo?"

The receptionist's lips purse. "I'm going on lunch break. Close the door on your way out."

Karin waits till the door slams before she steps around the desk once more and stares at the photo. Her father with his mining mates, and she doesn't know any of them. But why would she? Her father had never been forthcoming about his work. He was just Dad. While Mum waited on him and spent the rest of her time doing crosswords at the kitchen table.

There was supposed to be a happily ever after to reward them for their sacrifice. But with her father's death, they were just another family who had lived in a mining town once.

And now Karin is back, ostensibly for her friend's wedding, staring at the picture of a man who left his wife a widow and his children fatherless. Marlene Baxter: the sole beneficiary of a thirty-million-dollar payout—which she used to buy a non-descript house in a non-descript suburb in the city. A pale washed out mouse of a woman, who seemed confused about the idea that life was for living, waiting out her days for God know what, while her children attended private schools and wore fancy uniforms with boater hats and striped blazers.

During school holidays, with the small house bursting at the seams, Karin and her brothers would laugh and play board games and drink milkshakes out of metal tins and blow bubbles in the bottom. And there was no one to punch the sides of their heads for making a noise out of turn.

They agreed Dad had been a mean bastard. They also agreed that Mum brought it on herself by not standing up to him. It was hard to respect a woman who had no respect for herself.

Karin's brothers had gotten out as soon as they graduated university. But Karin stayed in Perth. For Mum. Although she wasn't sure why she bothered. If her mother couldn't help herself, why should she try to do it for her?

Karin followed her brothers to university and gotten an arts degree. Useless for anything except for storytelling. Journalism, maybe? Poking around in people's lives for a story to sell to some rag for a few bucks, if she was lucky.

It had been her dream forever, and if there was one thing watching her mother had taught her, it was that dreams mattered.

Her father had laughed at her in the early days. "Get real, darlin'. No one's going to bother with anything a girl like you can write. The real stories happen in places you can't imagine." And he laughed like he had said something funny.

Karin had looked at him, veiling the contempt she felt for the man she called her father, her disdain tempered by what she felt for her mouse of a mother who never fought back.

And then he was dead.

Uncle Bernie, one-time union boss for the mines, and who had been living rich in the city for years, had come to see them.

There's money, he said. Thirty million. But Karin's mother had pushed the news away like she didn't want to know.

Uncle Bernie had left, shrugging his shoulders like she was batshit crazy. The money was never mentioned again.

Karin sometimes wondered if she imagined that day. The unspoken words between her mother and her uncle.

It wasn't until she was away at university that she heard the rumours. Her best friends, Jessalyn Maskell and Rebecca Stanton, had cornered her and dragged her out into the marble pillared quadrangle one night and asked her if it was true. Had her father double-crossed his mates and sold out to the brass? Is that what had gotten him killed?

Now Karin stares at the picture hanging in the mine's office as if she can fathom the answer. Her eyes smart, but there is no way she will let the tears fall.

Is it possible his mates in the picture had decided to take justice into their own hands and that the fortune left to her mother in a fibro house in a non-descript suburb in the city was actually blood money? She doesn't want to think about it. But she cannot look away.

Karin feels the dog press against her jeans. She feels sick to the stomach that one of the men in the photo had gotten away with her father's murder. "You're right, Trouble. This place has bad vibes. Let's get out of here."

She shoves her phone into her pocket and clips the dog's leash as he follows her obediently out the door.

The fresh air, mingled with the dry burning heat, smacks her in the face and she pulls the collar of her shirt high to cover her neck. She needs to buy a wide-brimmed hat before the damn heat kills her.

"Come on, boy. It's time to get out of the sun for a while."

Chapter 3

KARIN looks towards the mountain with the Tourist Park at its base. It isn't far back to their van if they walk in a straight line. But it is mining land and off limits to the public. She and Trouble have no choice but to follow the road around the mine and she isn't sure Trouble's paws will cope with the heat of the bitumen.

"Wanna lift, luv?"

Her head snaps around and she finds herself staring at an old bloke with filthy leather gloves shoved in the waistband of his jeans, his thumbs hooked over the buckle of his belt. His eyes are mean even though he is smiling.

"Nev Shultz. Knew yer old man."

Trouble growls deep in his throat and Karin calms him with her hand. "Thanks. We're okay to walk," she replies, ignoring the relationship he proffers as introduction. Then she looks closer and stops. "I saw you in the photo in the office. You were standing next him. You were his friend."

The old man says nothing, merely looks at her through bloodshot eyes.

"What made you all turn on him?"

"Your old man thought he was the big shot. Started hobnobbin' it with the brass. The blokes didn't like it."

"And you?"

Nev shrugs. "I was used to his highfalutin' ideas. He was always travelling about the place. Measuring this. Timing that. He thought he'd save the brass money. Keeping the trains 24/7 was his big fuckin' brainwave."

"Was he right? How long does it take to stop a train and get it going again?"

"Don't matter. The boys didn't like it. It was their livelihoods he was screwing with. And they told him so. Gave him the choice."

"Someone would have come up with the idea eventually. Why not my father?"

"They would've been better bringing someone in from the outside. Instead, they sent yer old man to America. There was no stoppin' him after that. They even gave him a fuckin' promotion. The union tried to stop him. His own fuckin' brother. They came to blows, brother against brother, worker against brass." Nev spits in the dirt, and the dog gives another low growl.

Karin eyes the man silently. She knows how this town works. Management living in an enclave, backs circled, protecting each other. She thinks of the overpass. How close it is to where the bosses lived. Is that where her father had been the night he died? Had he fallen off the overpass and onto the tracks in front of a train?

"Then there was a downturn in the market. Layoffs. By the time things started to pick up, plans were underway to automate and there was no stoppin' yer old man then. Oh, it was all hush-hush. If word had gotten out the stock market would've gone crazy."

"And by the time it was announced, my father was dead."

"Funny thing that. Yer old man did all the hard yakka, but he wasn't around for the big payday."

Karin thinks of the thirty million dollars in her mother's bank account. "People got rich out of my father's technology."

"Rich." There is a bitter tone to Nev's laugh. "Darlin', they're all fuckin' billionaires."

"Billionaires? As in retired with the billions?"

"No fuckin' way. Once you get to that level of reach it's not about the money anymore. It's about the power. Look at Gina Rinehart. Makes money every second the clock ticks over from Pilbara ore.

Doesn't have to lift a finger and she's a fuckin' hero. Follow the money and you'll find the power," Nev says, a mean gleam in his eye. "Didn't your fancy fuckin' university education teach yer anything?"

Karin makes a mental note to find out how the old man knows so much about her.

"Besides, it's not yer old man's death that started it," Nev says cryptically. "It goes back a whole lot further than that."

The old man is talking in circles and Karin's brain is on overload. She is not sure if he is a little crazy.

She meets his yellow-eyed gaze. "Thank you for your offer of a lift," she says. "But me and my dog would rather walk."

"Suit yerself. Long walk back to the Tourist Park. An' I suggest ya take care. Trucks go mighty fast around here, and some might not be happy that yer back askin' yer damn fool questions."

She doesn't bother asking how he knows where she is staying, just like she doesn't ask how he knows she has been on the overpass.

She turns to leave, then hesitates. "Just one thing."

He turns as he climbs into his mine vehicle and looks at her.

"When did the automated trains start running?"

"A smart girl like you could Google stuff like that."

She nods. "I could."

"Which makes me think yer asking for another reason." He pulls himself into the vehicle and slams the door. She thinks that is the end of their conversation, until he lowers the window. "Be careful wearing red when yer out and about," he says. "Trains shut down for red."

The window closes and he backs the vehicle out with a loud revving sound. The wheels spin in the dirt as he drives off in the opposite direction to the town.

Chapter 4

BACK at the Tourist Park, she turns the aircon in the van to twenty-two degrees and pours herself icy water from the fridge. Trouble pushes past her and helps himself to gulps of water from his bowl, before flopping at the foot of the bed and closing his eyes.

Karin piles a couple of pillows high on the bed, kicks off her shoes and props herself against the headboard, the cold blast of the aircon slowly bringing down her core body temperature. Note to self: forty-five degrees is too fucking hot to be playing detective. Which reminds her of the old man's comment about brother against brother.

She pulls out her phone and flicks through her contacts till she finds who she is looking for. She waits while the phone connects.

"Uncle Bernie?"

"Hello, darlin'. How are you going up there in the heat?"

"Hot," she returns, forcing a laugh as she shares pleasantries. "Tell me about the trains," she says. 'People here seem reluctant to talk."

"That'd be on account of your Dad."

"Thought so."

"Be careful about the questions you ask," Bernie says softly. "There are people with long memories, and some have got a lot to lose."

"Their loss, my gain, apparently."

"Not if you're dead like your old man."

"About that," she says softly. "I saw a picture of him and his crew over at the mine just now. He was their hero, Uncle Bernie. They idolized him. I could see it in their eyes."

There is a pause at the other end of the line, and Karin can almost hear her uncle changing gears. "You know that old saying about pictures painting a thousand words?" he says slowly. "It's a fucking lie. You can make anything look good in a picture. You saw what you wanted to see, darling girl. You saw your father as a hero. But that's only part of the truth."

"Coming back has reminded me of things I'd forgotten," she said. "When we were little, Dad was always laughing. Until he stopped. What made him stop laughing? Why did Dad change?"

"Those places do things to a man's head," her uncle says. "They make you think you can be something that you're not. All that isolation and wide-open spaces can make a man go crazy. Or it can make him think he's more than he is."

"The article I found at the library today called him a legend among men."

"There was that," Bernie agrees. "But there was also the other side. The side where he sold out his mates to the brass."

"He sold out his mates?"

She hears the old man clear his throat before he continues, "So rumour had it."

"You were there, Uncle Bernie. You lived here back in the day. What did you think?"

"I saw a bloke out of out of his depth. I saw a man who thought he was bigger than he was. Like our old man before him. The firstborn son of the firstborn son." There is a pause, as if her uncle is contemplating what to say next. "Did he ever mention Mulga Plains Station? It was in our family for generations. Our father and his father before him worked sheep first, and later, cattle. It wasn't until things went bad that me and Jimbo got jobs at the mine, while the old man slogged his guts out on land that was as brutal as anywhere can be in a drought."

"I didn't know," Karin says. "Mum never said anything."

"She wouldn't. Trying to protect you and your brothers, probably. It was a bad time in all our lives. But the mine was good to us, and we got out of it without going bankrupt."

"You sold the station?"

"You could call it that." Karin can hear the bitterness in his voice. "Or you could say it was stolen from us."

Karin doesn't know what to say. "I always thought Dad was a railway man, through and through."

"He probably was in the end, but in the beginning our dreams were much bigger than that. Jimbo's more than mine. We were going to be cattle barons. Back in the day it was the thing to be sent south to get a good education. University and all that. Your father took to it like a duck to water. Came out with a Royal Engineering Degree and big ideas about expanding the station. He reckoned permanent sources of water were there for the taking. Me, I didn't hold such aspirations. I was happy just to live my life in the wide-open spaces. But neither of us got what we wanted in the end."

Karin thinks of the article that lists her father's qualifications. She had been surprised to see the number of letters after his name. He had followed up his degree with post-doctoral studies in AgTech.

"Did Dad use his engineering qualification at the mine, or was he always going back to work the station?"

"A bit of both, at first. The brass put him in the Railways Division and gave him a fancy title, but really it was just to sideline him. Until the stupid bastard suggested automating the trains. Said it would speed up delivery of the ore tenfold to the Port in Dampier if the trains didn't have to stop and start all the time to change drivers. He even went to the States and saw how it worked over there and brought the technology back. He had some grand fucking plan to automate the whole Pilbara. Which is ironic, because that's exactly what happened. But not with your father's name on it."

"The money," Karin says softly. "I overheard you talking with Mum after Dad died. You said something about thirty million dollars, but Mum never mentioned it again."

"It should have been thirty billion," Bernie says quietly. "But there was nothing in writing. Your old man was a trusting bastard, and the brass took him for everything he had—including the family farm, it turns out. The funny thing is the blokes hated him in the end, too. Thought he sold them out."

"Because automating the trains would have taken their jobs?"

"Truth. I was the union rep, and they came to me with their complaints about my own brother. What was I supposed to do? I did what I could to warn him, but the blokes took justice in their own hands. At least, that's what was rumoured later. I was with your Mum when the coppers came to tell us that your Dad's brains were splattered all over the railway track. Imagine your Mum having to pack up and take you kids south after that. She always looked up to him. He was her fucking hero. She was never the same afterwards."

"Do you think it was rough justice that got him killed?"

"Like I said, I didn't ask then, and I suggest you don't ask now. It's been too long, and if you start dragging things up, who knows what the consequences will be. Take my word on this one, Karin. Keep your mouth shut and your head down, and get out of there as soon as your friend's wedding is over. For all our sakes."

Karin holds the phone as it goes dead.

Her uncle has hung up on her. Which leaves her—where, exactly? She didn't know what the truth was before they talked; she has no idea what it is now. But one thing for certain is that her uncle has said all he intends to say.

Is that why her mother has never touched the money? Because it is tainted with her father's blood?

Was her father a hero or a villain?

Her first day back in town and already she has more questions than answers.

Small towns and their secrets run deep. If she wants to get anywhere and find out anything, she will have to get a whole lot smarter. Like Uncle Bernie said, there are people that know things in this town, and they're watching her. Nev Schultz had said as much this afternoon.

What were his words again? A smart girl like her. At the time she thought he'd been talking about her being an outsider, but she wonders if her uncle is right. If Nev was warning her to be careful who she trusted.

Coming back for her best friend's wedding might not have been the smartest idea after all. But she's here now—and she's determined to do justice to her father's memory, regardless of her jumbled emotions where he is concerned.

If Uncle Bernie is right, and thirty million dollars is a drop in the ocean to what her father is really owed, then there will be people who will do anything to stop her finding out the truth.

But she isn't her father's daughter for nothing. If there's one thing his money has done, it's giving her the best education that money could buy—and even better connections. The people in this town are not the only ones with friends in high places. If she is lucky, that will work to her advantage.

Until it doesn't.

And by then she will be ready.

Chapter 5

SHE leaves Trouble asleep in the cool of the van and walks past Reception to the T-intersection of Happy Valley Road. She turns right and follows the signs to the fenced cemetery, where she steps over scattered yellow and white cockatoo feathers and lets her gaze wander around the manicured graves.

She finds her father's headstone easily enough. It is a metre-square headstone made of grey polished tiles, standing sentinel in a line of low marbled headstones that adorn the surrounding graves. There are faded bottle-green plastic chairs at the head of each grave, like someone used to visit once, and plastic flowers long past their use-by dates crammed into tin cans perch tiredly on several of the graves.

Her father's grave has neither a chair nor plastic flowers. Instead, there timber bench carved out of Jarrah with a metal nameplate that read; *Amicos tuos prope tene*

Inimicos tuos prope tene. Hold your friends close and your enemies closer, she translates. *Donated by the Railway Workers Union of WA.*

On a tile in the centre of the headstone her father's name is written in raised gold letters.

James Reginald Baxter,
born 15.4.1958, died 26.6.1993
Devoted husband
Loving father
Beloved brother
In loving memory

She smiles faintly. Devoted husband of a loyal wife who has no name. Two sons and a daughter. A brother who hated his guts.

Sorely missed by all who knew him

She drops onto the bench and crosses knee over the other like she has been invited. "It seems we've got the local tongues wagging, you and I."

She leans forward ad brushes her fingers across the gold lettering. A covering of red dirt that is worn like a favourite shirt over most things in the Pilbara comes away on her hand. "Your old friend, Nev, is angry that I'm here. Maybe he had hoped it was all over, whatever it was you pair have done."

"Did you mean to end up here, Dad? Immortalised in the shadow of the mountain because people thought you dreamed too big? Uncle Bernie for one. Did you know he's pissed that you lost the family farm? It seems he had dreams of his own and he wasn't happy that you sold him out."

But pissed enough to kill his own brother? Karin isn't sure. Although she has sometimes wondered if Uncle Bernie hadn't coveted his brother's wife. In the years since her father's death, Uncle Bernie was solicitous, for sure. Her mother had seemed not so much indifferent but aware that life went on regardless.

"Mum's been stuck in a time warp since you died, did you know? Trapped by a promise of a happily ever after she never got to claim. Did you ask her if it was okay? Or was the money supposed to make it all worth it for her?"

On impulse, she gets out her phone and sends a photo of the grave to her mother. Her poor fucking mother. There had been no easy escape for her. She lives out her days wondering what went wrong.

"About the money," she continues. "Mum never touched it, you know. I always wondered why."

She waits, as if her father will provide an answer. One that makes better sense than blood money.

"You laughed at my storytelling, ridiculed me. Said the stories happen where I can't go. But I'm here now, and my mind is working overtime. You were right about one thing. Nobody's talking. Not even Uncle Bernie. But they're watching. That's a start."

She looks over at an old wrought iron fence, neatly mown around the outside, grass high as her waist inside. If there is a headstone within, it's long been forgotten.

There is no chair at her father's grave, but someone has kept the high-gloss grey tiles polished, and the gold cursive writing free (for the most part) of

"Who visits you, Dad? Is it possible you still have friends here after fifteen years? Uncle Bernie said they hated you. That you sold them out. Did you do that, Dad? Did you go over to the dark side?"

She frowns. She doesn't even know what the dark side means in this godforsaken place. Thirty million is a good payout in anyone's language, and had her father lived, it would have kept him and Mum for the rest of their lives. In the city. Away from the scene of any crimes committed in his name. And far from the dust and dirt and men full of resentment for a man that was once one of their own.

"The write-up in the local paper said you were a legend. They called you a man of vision, a man with a great brain and a meticulous eye for detail. That men looked up to you. Respected you. Until they didn't."

"I can understand why you would go to America. It was where the technology was. You brought that knowledge back and you put it to work for those that employed you. Streamlined the process. The biggest automated train network ever built.

"It was all about your colossal ego. You may have lost the family farm, but you put your name to a rail network bigger and better than anything in the world. Except then you died."

Karin's phone vibrates and she pulls it from her pocket. Her mother has sent a message. Her mother who never calls, let alone sends an SMS.

Say hello for me 😁

Her mother has sent a laughing emoji to the man she had sworn to love, honour and obey.

Not anymore, apparently.

Karin sighs. Has she underestimated her mother all these years? Had gaining her freedom been enough? Knowing her husband will never escape the place they had called home. Now she lives a nondescript life in a nondescript place, with—finally—the freedom to do as she pleases.

Karin smiles slowly. Thirty million in a Commonwealth Bank passbook in a shoebox at the bottom of her wardrobe. Never updated for interest. The money never spent. Some fucking name for freedom.

She shoots off another message.

You won, didn't you?

You waited your turn and you took it

And now you're free

No wonder her mother hadn't wanted her to come back here and stir things up again. Risking the life she has so carefully curated. Grieving widow seeing out her days in oblivion, her only pleasures the Friday night raffle at the local bowling club and Sunday lunch with her daughter when she is in town.

The phone vibrates.

Her mother has sent an angel face emoji.

Karin smiles and silently wishes her mother ongoing invisibility. Because whoever had ended her father's life has not ended the story. Uncle Bernie knows that. So does her mother. And so does Nev Schultz, with his mean glare and mocking tone. As if he knows Karin will never know what really happened to her father in the dark in a mining town in the middle of nowhere. Because she is female, she has no access to a world where men do deals with the shaking of hands and spits in the dirt while they take a leak behind a Pilbara ghost gum on the rail access road to the coast. Where secrets sail on the tide and all trace is washed away in the sand.

She thinks back to her mother's reaction when Karin had told her she was coming up for Jess's wedding. They had been eating dinner. Her mother had looked at her and gone back to her roast beef and gravy, forking neat mouthfuls through smiling lips, saying nothing.

The cunning old bitch.

Karin makes a mental note not to underestimate the woman she has felt sorry for all these years.

Nothing is as it seems, Uncle Bernie had said.

No fucking kidding.

She looks up again at her father's grave. "The least I can do is rewrite the legend and get you the recognition you deserve," she says. "Old Nev can try and stop me. And Bernie. With Mum in the city and the boys on the other side of the world, I'm the only chance you've got left. Do you want me to tell your story, Dad? To make you the hero of your own legend? Do you want me to go where you told me I couldn't?"

His silence is telling.

"Challenge accepted," she says softly. "For a start, nobody has ever been charged with your death."

Death by misadventure.

Things going wrong in the night. A train accident in the footnotes of a mountain where big explosions are the only thing that matter. Sold to the highest bidder on international stock exchanges and shipped to countries where records of tonnage are buried in tape so red it will take Karin forever to untangle the mess.

Untraceable. Like the pissing deal behind the tree that kicked off their billions in the first place.

Oral history. Passed down through generations. Men of Iron. Their exploits told to children as warnings to make them behave if they want their own happily ever after.

Karin's happily ever after is tied directly to the silence of the man dead in his grave at her feet.

She spit-polishes her reflection in the grey-tiled wall that is her father's headstone. "Did you know, Dad, that women can piss standing up nowadays, too?"

Nobody wants to tell her the story of her father's death. Explorers charting unexplored mountain ranges in the far-from-the-city northwest. The Pilbara, the stuff of mining legends, a vast open land there for the taking. Blast the cave-art to smithereens. Blown-up evidence of pre-possession. Leave no witnesses. No lies to tell. Last one turns out the lights.

And so, the warnings begin. Does she really want to risk more deaths—including her own—by asking questions?

Uncle Bernie warning her away with cryptic references to letting dogs lie. Old Nev and his glaring eyes and talk of disappearing into the dark. And Mum. Her weapon of choice is silence, accompanied by an angel emoji.

The questions are hers alone to ask and, vested interests aside, none of anyone's business.

It's a matter of asking the right questions to the right people.

And protecting her back.

"You were a genius, Dad. More interested in your technology and how to make it work. You just forgot to think about money it would make. Who stood to benefit the most from your genius?"

A money train is snaking through her brain just as surely as the ore trains hauled their loads across the Pilbara ranges. Follow the money to the sea, and across the oceans to offshore bank accounts. And beyond. Untraceable, so they say. Until someone does. And there is all hell to pay.

"Your friend Nev says *follow the money, girlie* like it is an insult. The same way you spoke about my writing. But thanks to him, I've worked out where to start looking."

She bows her head in acknowledgement to the father she has loved but never really known. And leaves the cemetery the way she has come.

As she walks out the gate a flutter of movement from the window of a donga in the adjoining construction camp catches her eye.

Someone has been watching.

She smiles softly and continues walking. She has a hen's night to attend and her best friends to celebrate with. Tomorrow is soon enough to begin her search for the person—or persons—who killed her father and think they have gotten away with it.

But Karin knows there is no such thing as karma.

It is time for the bad guys to pay—and she intends to be there when they do.

Chapter 6

KARIN pulls a pair of lightweight jeans and white polo shirt from the overhead cupboard. Trouble is already curled up asleep for the night, chasing imaginary rabbits across a paddock.

Bridesmaid's duty. It's what she's here for. She walks to the other end of the van, not bothering to turn the light on in the tiny bathroom. She pulls on her jeans, drops the polo over her head, and applies a light lip-gloss as a concession to make-up. Last, she twists her ponytail into a loose bun at her nape and secures it with a hair-tie, then heads for the door.

She slips into her Merrills, checks the dog's water bowl, and locks the door softly behind her.

It's a beautiful night for a walk. She cuts behind the cart track and follows Old South Road to the Golfie. It takes her half an hour, but it gives her a chance to empty her head. It's time to tuck the problem of her father's death away until later. Tonight is about old friends catching up and setting Jess on her marriage journey.

Karin counts stars as she walks.

Bec and Jess, her old school friends. The things they had gotten up to out the back of the Golfie while their parents had been inside. Their fathers delivered Fantas and Smiths Chips, and the girls talked boys, and the escapes they would make as soon as they were old enough.

Funny. She is the only one that followed through.

She sees the lights of the golf club as she swings past tee beds built on mounds and sand greens scraped with oil. How many tournaments had been played on the outback course, where neat fairway drives could end up anywhere if they hit a rock? Men chasing little white balls around a paddock had never made much sense to her, but out here, where fairways are carved into the landscape like footprints made with hobnail boots, it makes even less sense.

Had her father played golf? Her days in the city had taught her that the golf course was a place of deals over fairway shots and pitches to the green, sealed with handshakes at the flag. Boardrooms were reserved for crafting prospectus notes for investors with more money than questions about mines thousands of kilometres from the nearest legal oversight.

Karin pushes open the steel-mesh gate of the clubhouse and turns left onto the covered verandah with its wooden tables and plastic chairs. A floor-to-ceiling black Sony speaker is blasting out music choreographed through a wide television screen of music video clips.

So far no one dancing.

She feels the heels of her shoes stick to the concrete with too many nights of spilled beers and her gaze sweeps over cigarette butts brushed to the side of the concrete by the four a.m. broom. Friday nights at the Golfie are a regular thing, and it won't be long before the place is packed with workers at end of shift looking for a feed and few coldies before they hit the sack, mingled with the Friday night raffle crowd.

A cordoned off section is set up with white cotton tablecloths and brightly coloured bougainvillea branches woven into centrepieces. The plastic chairs in this section are tied with hot pink balloons, except one, which is decorated with white velvet and an artificial back shaped like a throne. Champagne buckets filled with ice adorn the tables and there are trays of glasses ready to go on a bench in one corner. Bec's doing, she guesses, noting the hot-pink serviettes shaped like swans, piled high alongside brown paper bags festooned with pink ribbons, gold-calligraphed nametags and, if she was to hazard a guess, truth-or-dare cards stuffed inside.

Alcohol, games, and a gaggle of women unfettered from their responsibilities ready to party. *What happens at the hen's night stays at the hen's night.* It's been a long time since she has let her hair down and had fun for the sake of it.

Jess's hen's party has been hyped up as the event of the season, the Maskell name ensuring that everything between now and the wedding will be written up in the city papers. *No pressure*, Karin thinks, as she heads towards her friends.

Jess is sitting on the velvet throne, wearing a veil and a gold-lettered sash that says *Bride*. Bec sits to her left. The two women have their heads together, talking animatedly.

"We came early to snag a spot," Bec says as Karin drops a kiss on each of their heads and sits on Jess's other side. Bec pours Karin a glass of Moet and passes it to her before topping up Jess's glass. "The bus will be here soon with the gang, and then it'll be standing room only."

Karin picks up her glass and sips. "So, this is it." She smiles at Jess. "Party time."

Jess nods, toppling her veil. She pushes it back onto her head. "I can't believe you walked. We could have picked you up on the way."

Karin shrugs. "You know me. Independent and all that."

Her friends laugh. "Good to see some things haven't changed," Jess says with a grin. "I can't tell you how glad I am you came back for my wedding. Are you settled in at the Tourist Park?"

Karin nods. "Trouble's snoring his head off as we speak. I left him on guard duty."

Bec holds up her glass. "Now that we're all here, it's time to get serious. To Jess."

"To Jess." Karin raises her glass. "I can't believe you're really tying the knot. To a man with a title, no less."

Jess shrugs. "What can I say. I'm irresistible." She fluffs her veil and makes a show of holding out her hand, revealing an engagement ring with a single pink diamond. "Consider me taken."

"An Argyle diamond. I'm impressed."

"Nothing but the best for the joining of two dynasties," Jess says, dropping her hand to her glass and sculling her champagne.

Bec winks at Karin from across the table. "The deal isn't sealed until the papers are signed. There's hope for the rest of us mere mortals yet."

Jess smiles, but there is a shadow in her gaze. "True love can't be thwarted by mere paperwork. The handsome prince is mine."

"Here's to happily ever after to your fairytale," Karin toasts. "And recalcitrant pieces of paper."

"I'll drink to that." Jess holds her glass out to Bec. "Pieces of paper be damned, I say. Especially ones that go mysteriously missing when you need them."

Karin frowns. "Problems in paradise?"

"Nothing that can't be taken care of." Jess fusses with her ring. "Tonight is about us celebrating, right?"

Bec shakes her head at Karin behind Jess's back as she stands to get another bottle of champagne.

Karin takes the hint that now isn't the time. "I've come a long way for this party. Let's do it." She holds her glass up to her friend.

Jess clinks her glass lightly. "I'll drink to that, too."

The women laugh as Bec returns with another bottle and drops into her chair. "To happily ever after," she says as she pours. "Do you think six cases of champagne is enough?"

"We can always move on to cocktails." Jess lifts her glass. "And don't forget your Bridezilla Punch, Bec."

Karin laughs, and soon they are discussing the latest rage in wedding cocktails. "How about Blue Margaritas for something blue?" she suggests.

"Bachelorette Mojitos," Bec one-ups her. "For us bridesmaids."

"I've heard that Blushing Bride Bellinis are a must," Karin says, poker-faced.

Jess nods solemnly. "Virgin Martinis," she says. "For the...err...virgins among us."

They are laughing and already a little tipsy when the courtesy bus pulls up at the gate. A dozen or so women pour out and head towards them.

As introductions flow, Karin smiles politely and wonders how she will remember everyone. Most are friends from Jess's work. A few are Bec's artist friends. Karin is the only one from somewhere else. She leans back into her chair with her champagne and lets the conversation flow around her.

Then the music ramps up and her peace is over.

"Come on, you pair. Let's get this party moving." Jess drags her and Bec to their feet to the sound of B52's "Rocklobster" and train-dances them around the verandah to the cheers of patrons enjoying the spectacle of one of the town's brass letting her hair down with such abandon on her hen's night.

Karin gives up trying to maintain her dignity and twirls and spins around with strangers who sing "Girls Just Wanna Have Fun" in a bad parody of Cyndi Lauper. She links arms with strangers and hugs and kisses and laughs until she is dizzy and hungry and more than a little drunk. The concrete floor is a mess of party poppers and streamers, and Karin wonders when food will arrive to soak up the alcohol she has consumed.

As "Rasputin" blasts through the speakers, Bec leans into her and they hip-bump. "Let's catch up tomorrow and discuss our bridesmaids' duties."

"Sounds like a plan. But what about tonight? Have we got to make a speech or anything?" The idea fills her with dread, even drunk.

Bec winks. "All taken care of."

"Please tell me we're not going to have a stripper?" The only thing she can think of that's worse than slurring her words in public is ogling a naked man's body and enjoying it.

"Don't tell me you've gone prudish on us? Naked men used to be your thing." Bec shakes her head like she knows Karin is secretly hoping to tuck fifty-dollar notes into a man's G-string.

"Only in my dreams," returns Karin, secretly mortified that her friend is right.

Bec stumbles into her and laughs as she looks over her shoulder. "Maybe tonight your dreams will come true."

Karin follows her gaze and starts. "You didn't tell me Lukah was back in town."

Jess dances over. "Surprise, darling." She is drunk and throws her arms around her two best friends. "Who knows? You might be next in the marriage stakes. From what I remember you two were tight."

"We were sixteen."

"He's single," Bec whispers theatrically into her ear.

"A single man in a mining town, what a surprise." Karin feels the heat rise in her face. She is uncomfortable with the attention, especially as it comes straight after her fifty-dollar G-string-tucking fantasy. Lukah in a G-string is too much for her brain and she closes her eyes.

"Brave up," Jess stage-whispers as she dances off. "He's spotted you."

Karin watches as her childhood sweetheart, beer in hand, locks gazes with her. A slow smile spreads across his face.

He mouths, "Hello, you."

Bec shoves her forward. "Go and say hello, idiot."

"Don't have to," Karin mutters, wondering if it is undignified to turn tail and run.

Too late, she realizes. Lukah Sorreli, the last person she expected to see here, is smiling and heading her way.

Chapter 7

"**D**ANCE?"

Karin looks at him, feigning surprise. "Lukah?"

He grins. "One and the same. Come on, chica. Let's see if we've still got it."

With the encouragement of her friends, Karin finds herself moving towards the makeshift dancefloor as ABBA's *Dancing Queen* lights up the TV screen.

"Ready," he whispers, and swings her into the middle of the dance floor.

Without quite realising how, she executes moves she didn't know her body still remembered. Lukah's hands are locked firmly with hers and he is smiling down at her.

He pulls her close, then deftly slides her between his legs and pulls her back up for a lift, his hands catching her hips as he steadies her in his arms. "Having fun?"

She looks into his eyes and bursts out laughing. "*Dirty Dancing*, each your heart out."

He links his arms behind her waist and pulls her close. "Miss me?"

"It's been a few years," she observes dryly. "Like about ten."

"Try fourteen years, three months, eight days, sixty-three minutes and—" he looks at his wristwatch, "—fourteen seconds."

She pulls back. "You made that up."

"Maybe." He pulls her closer, using his body to shield her from the more exuberant moves of those dancing around them.

Karin realises she has missed him, the way he looked out for her, how he was always there when she needed him, and often when she didn't know she did. "What made you come back?"

"A job came up. I thought you might return one day looking for answers, and I wanted to be here when you did."

"You always said you wanted to be a policeman when you grew up. Are you?"

He nods. "And you're a writer, just like you said you'd be. I read your stuff sometimes."

It's too much for her to take in on an empty stomach, and she blurts out the one question she doesn't want to know the answer to. "Are you married?" Who is she kidding, it all she wants to know.

She feels the rumble of his chest and knows that he knows what she's thinking, just like he's always known, damn him. "An interesting question to start with."

"To start with what?" She is playing with fire. She blames the champagne.

"I asked you to dance, not to fuck, sweetheart."

She pulls away slightly and looks up at him through half-closed eyes. "Pity. From memory, you were good."

This time it's him who pulls away. He looks down at her, laughter in his eyes. "You still fighting the world, chica?"

"Never stopped."

She turns and walks off the dance floor, expecting him to let go of her. He doesn't. He follows, his hand still firmly entwined with hers. She's not sure how she feels about him assuming a relationship that no longer exists. She swings away from the group of women, where the champagne is flowing freely, and heads towards the open doorway and fresh air.

"Good idea," he says. "Time to cool down after all that heat."

She tugs her hand out of his. "Stop being slutty," she says waspishly, like it wasn't her who upped the awareness between them in the first place. "You're the one who mentioned fucking."

"You were thinking it. I saw it in your eyes, just you like you saw it in mine."

"Too much wine. What's your excuse? No, don't answer that." She opens the gate and leads them out onto the golf course, away from the lights and prying eyes of her friends.

Coming back to the town where she grew up, she had made sure she was mentally prepared in every way. Except one. And he is standing with her in the moonlight under a starry sky talking sex like it is small talk between them. The man that was once her childhood sweetheart has matured into a hot magnet of temptation.

I cannot afford the distraction, she tells herself, then forgets to listen to her warning.

As they stroll along the first fairway, she ponders the irony of the boy she had a crush on fifteen years ago—and whose body promises delicious sex now if only she gives the word—is a local policeman and the one person in the whole town she must avoid at all costs. The Lukah of old had been protective, overly so, and now she is about to put herself in danger by flushing out a killer.

Hey, Lukah, let's fool around a bit, but try not to care too much because what I'm about to do may not end well and I don't want you to get hurt—or worse—because of me.

Sure, as if Lukah will accept her words at face value and head back inside like they are people who knew each other once.

"I didn't come dressed to lie in the dirt and look up at the sky with an old friend," she says.

"I don't remember that ever stopping us."

"We were kids. And did what all kids do. Sneak out and grope each other away from watching eyes."

He stops and turns her gently towards him. "So now that we're all grown up you want a comfy bed, is that what you're telling me? Baxter, I'm disappointed in you."

He grins down at her, teasing, and she wants nothing more than to sink to the rocky ground and fuck him with her on top. He is right about one thing. She is too old for rocks digging into her back as he drives her to oblivion and neither of them have come prepared like they used to in the old days: with picnic rug, a supply of condoms, and water bottles to spare.

She changes the subject. "Are there many of the old gang still around town?"

"Not many. Jess, Bec, me, and Aldo that I know of. Then there's the occasional comment on Facebook from escapees saying how much they miss the place and the good old days. I'm taking it from your change of topic we're not about to relive a few of those memories ourselves."

"I didn't come here prepared for you," Karin admits. Her blood pulses hrough her veins. He is going to kiss her. And she is going to let him.

She wonders briefly if it is one of the reasons she has come back. To find what she hasn't been able to find in the city.

Trust.

She trusts Lukah.

And she has no problem kissing him under the stars. Or, if she is honest, making love with him. Except...

"You're wondering if I've got a place, aren't you?"

She knows what he is asking. She just isn't quite sure if she is ready to go there yet. Memories of moonlight romps and stolen kisses and long slow lovemaking with the night air caressing her bare skin as he strips her T-shirt over her head and tenderly kisses each of her breasts like she is queen and he her consort.

Nope, definitely not ready.

"I don't think we should start anything we can't handle." She turns in his arms, leans against him and looks across at the mountain. "You climb up there anymore?"

He spreads his legs wide and settles her more comfortably. She feels the shape of him pressed against her and her body responds by relaxing into his easy embrace.

"Nah, too old for that kind of shit. I like my women in a comfy bed nowadays." He rests his chin on her head. "But only if they're willing."

She likes the new Lukah. Mellow, honest, and still hers if she wants him. There's never been any secrets between them, and she isn't sure how he'll deal with her secrets now. And she doesn't want to hurt him with her lies.

"Maybe one day," she says. "When all this is over."

"Don't go there."

She doesn't pretend to misunderstand. "It's why I'm here, or at least one of the reasons." She pulls gently out of his arms. "Time I got home, I think."

He drops a kiss on her nose. "I'll walk part-way with you."

It is his way of compromise, and she nods. "Should we go back and say our goodbyes?"

"They won't even know we're gone, and if they do, they'll congratulate themselves for getting us back together."

"Are we back together, Lukah? Or is the night playing tricks with us?"

"Let's walk," he says, taking her hand. "And we can decide the answer to that one on the way."

Chapter 8

THEY walk in companionable silence.

They have been this way before, many times, and she already has an inkling where he is taking her. When the water tanks come into view, looming ahead of them in stark contrast to the shadows of the mountain, she shivers. The mountain has always looked more sinister on the dark side of the moon, as if its shadows hold secrets that it has no intention of revealing.

It is where they used to come when they wanted to be alone. Some people had a song. They had this place.

She doesn't resist when Lukah stops and pulls her down onto her arse. He doesn't let go of her hand and instead tugs her closer. His legs are crossed, and he rests their hands on his thigh. He massages the inside of her hand with his thumb.

"You can see for miles," she says softly.

"I come here when I need to think. It was our spot, remember?"

Karin pretends to give the idea consideration, but she is unsettled. In front of them, the train tracks curve around onto a bridge that passes over the road back to the Tourist Park. Her gaze follows the tracks past a big white shed, which looks like a giant gazebo but is really the place where the trains are shunted when they need fixing. On the other side of the tracks is the cul-de-sac where Jess's construction company has its offices and stores its machinery. The tracks continue and disappear through the underpass where she and Trouble had been standing earlier that day. She is once again looking over to where her father's body was found, only this time from the opposite direction.

She feels Lukah watching her and turns to him. "This is the second time today I've looked at the place where it happened."

Lukah doesn't pretend to misunderstand. "The Karin Baxter I knew would never have rested until she had all the answers."

"The Karin Baxter you knew hated her father's guts."

"You were angry at him. Angry at all of us, from what I recall."

"Maybe," she says. "Mum acted all indifferent when I told her I was coming back. Today, when I was at the cemetery, I sent her a picture of his grave and she sent back an angel face emoji."

Lukah smiles softly. "You think she's forgotten about him. That she's happy he's gone."

"An angel face means innocence. Like she hasn't got anything to hide."

"Maybe she hasn't. Maybe your Dad's death was an accident like they say."

"She has a bank account with thirty million dollars in it. Untouched. Explain that."

"You think it's blood money, don't you? And that's why you can't let it go."

Karin sees the policeman frown forming on his forehead and that he is curious. Good. She wants him on her side.

"I met an old bloke today. Nev Schultz," she says. "He said he was an old friend of my father. He said Dad's mates had a grudge against him and that his death was a pub crawl gone wrong."

"And you don't believe him because…?"

Karin rests her head on his shoulder. "Thirty million is a lot of money to turn up in a bank account for no reason."

"It is that. But hey, compared to the real money they're making around this place it's peanuts. Did you know that Rinehart and Rio make two and a half million bucks an hour from the ore being carted to the coast? And that's just their share of the royalties. Compared to that kind of money, thirty million is nothing."

"Thirty million and my father's life."

She feels the brush of his lips against her hair. "Whatever happens, chica, I'm here for you. I won't let anything bad happen on my watch."

At his words, Karin feels the tension in ease into something akin to a calm she hasn't felt since she arrived. She moves her head slightly to turn her face into his neck and rests her lips at his collarbone. "You smell nice."

"I'm glad you're here," he says softly, dropping a kiss onto her forehead, "With me, like this. But try not to get yourself killed over old grudges."

"You're the local constabulary. Wouldn't you hear if there were evil doings underfoot?"

"As far as I'm aware, it's all quiet around the place. Most of the wild west stuff happened back in the day. Nowadays, other than the never-ending court battle between Rinehart and Hammersley, the native title claims with Fortescue, Rio smashing the local rock art and trying to cover it up, and the lowering of the water table out at the Gorge, its business as usual."

"I thought I might contact a friend to see if they can trace the money."

"A friend, huh? Does that mean I have competition?"

Karin closes her teeth on his neck.

"Ouch."

"I'm not sure if you've heard, but a woman belongs to no man. We choose what we want and how we want it."

"You should give a talk at the local school while you're here," he replies. "We've got a bit of a misogyny problem with our young blokes, and it wouldn't hurt to remind our girls they have choices." He rubs his neck. "Unless you tell them to bite."

"Maybe I will. It's time girls learned it's okay to fight for what they want."

She thinks of her mother, who has never fought for anything, as far as Karin knows. So much for role models. If she had followed in her mother's footsteps, she'd be married with two kids by now and stuck in some godforsaken mining town eking out her days reading old copies of New Idea magazines and cutting out recipes for Saturday night dinners.

Karin looks down at the town. "We were lucky, weren't we? We grew up when it was okay to wander the streets and not come home till it was dark. Good times. The kids today must do it tough, with their Internet and their algorithms showing them stuff they shouldn't see and have less hope of understanding."

"You're going to make a great mother," he says with a chuckle. "Wanna make babies with me?"

Karin pulls back and looks into his eyes, her gaze speculative. "If I was going to make babies with anyone, you've certainly got the right genealogy, I guess."

"A romantic proposition if ever I heard one, Baxter." He pushes to his feet and holds his hand down to help her up. "I accept. Let's go."

She allows him to help her up, liking the idea of using his body for sex a little too much. "You can walk me to the corner. Then we go our separate ways, you home to your bed and me home to mine."

"Just like old times," he says wickedly. "I like it when you play hard to get. Adds a sense of anticipation."

"Anticipate away, but right now, I need sleep."

The going is easier downhill towards Mine Road. She slips a couple of times, and Lukah reaches out a steadying hand. Old friends walking home together just like old times. Who is she kidding? She wants him, and they aren't teenagers anymore.

Mt Nameless comes into view, distracting her. "Do you ever climb up there anymore?" She looks up at the mountain shrouded in the shadows of a scattered clouds.

"Jarndunmunha?" he asks softly. "I take all my girlfriends there."

The stab of jealousy is unexpected and Karin falters. "All of them? At once?"

"Haven't you heard? Harems are a thing nowadays?"

"I prefer reverse harems," she says. "Just saying."

"I don't like the idea of thinking of you with anyone else either. What have you done to me, witch? You've only been back five minutes and we're already talking babies."

"Stranger things have happened," she says. "Look at Jess. Who would have thought she'd marry into royalty?"

"Around here, she's the royalty. Grayson Kenneth Caddel, the Third, is the lucky one in that relationship."

Karin is reminded of Bec's warning earlier in the night. "You don't think it's a business arrangement, do you? A merging of dynasties?"

"If it is, it doesn't seem to be worrying Jess and Grayson too much. They're happy," he says softly. "Quit your worrying."

She comes to a halt at the railway crossing on Happy Valley Road. "It's my job to worry, apparently," she says. "As chief bridesmaid, I'm supposed to find the perfect place for the happy couple to exchange their vows. Bec has already organsied the reception at the Eco Retreat, with a three-piece orchestra and linen tablecloths and a hundred guests, but she left the location of the ceremony to me."

"My guess is you'll be spoilt for choice, Chica. It's not as if there's a shortage of clifftops out there."

"You don't get it. I haven't been out to Karijini in years, and I'm supposed to find the perfect sunset backlighting over a gorge. If I get it wrong, Bec will never forgive me. It can't just be any cliff or any gorge. It has to be the perfect one. And from what I remember, there are too many places to choose from."

He pulls her close and drops an arm over her shoulder. "Sounds like you could do with some help."

"You offering?" She turns into his chest and looks up, but her gaze gets no further than his lips.

He tilts his head forward. "You asking?"

Is she? Involuntarily, she rises on her toes and meets him halfway.

Their kiss is exploratory. Soft. Questioning. Like they know what they want, but there is no hurry. She likes the feel of his lips on hers and knows she can pull back at any time. But all that changes when Lukah deepens the kiss. Her knees give way and she is vaguely aware of his arms encircling her, holding her upright as her brain short-circuits and she can't remember to do anything other than kiss him back as he takes them closer to the abyss they've been flirting with all night.

It would be easy to stay here like this, glued together in the moonlight under the watchful gaze of the mountain, feeling things she'd buried long ago, but that the man who is kissing her knows intuitively how to light her fire, threatening combustion right here in the middle of the railway line, five hundred metres from the Tourist Park and safety of her van.

He pulls away slightly, breaking their kiss, a question in his eyes.

She takes the coward's way out and looks up at the mountain. "Jarndunmunha," she says. "Remember how we used to run up it?"

"You were always the one to set the challenge." The double-entendre is not lost on her.

"And you could never resist," she says, wondering if they're talking about the mountain or something else entirely. "You always used to let me win."

"I used to stay behind you so I could look at your arse."

"Only because I let you look."

"Of all the women in the world to be standing in the moonlight with tonight, I get stuck with a feminist."

"Just remember we feminists like our coffee strong. If you have a free day anytime soon I'll let you bring me coffee and take me swimming out at the Gorge."

"I'll check my roster and get back to you."

"It's a date. Thanks for walking me home."

"You don't want me to see you all the way?"

She hears the wistfulness in his voice and smiles. "Sorry to ruin your dreams, Lothario, but I think I can find my way down Happy Valley Road by myself."

"I suppose you can," he says forlornly. "Pity, I've always wanted to rock a rooftop van." He slips his arms around her waist. "Do one thing for me."

"Kiss you again? Sure." She puckers her lips into an exaggerated moue.

He takes the invitation and drops a quick kiss on her upturned lips. "Promise me you'll be careful."

She grins up at him. "Are you worried about me?"

"Have you got any idea about the paperwork that goes into a dead body?"

"You think someone wants me dead?"

"Not dead exactly. More warned off. If you want to tell me who you've been upsetting, I'm all ears."

She touches the side of her nose and offers him a conspiratorial wink. "Need to know," she says. "But if and when I need a tall dark handsome policeman, you'll be the first one I'll call."

"Put me on speed dial."

She pulls out of his arms and turns towards the caravan park. "Thanks for walking me home. Let me know about Karijini.

If he is watching, he will have the same view he got when they were kids. Her walking away and him left wanting more.

It had always been that way between them.

She wonders what it would be like if she stopped and let him catch her up. A happily ever after between them after all these years is not out of the realm of possibility and her step is light as she walks away from the man who captured her heart all those years and has been keeping it safe for her ever since.

Chapter 9

KARIN sits back in her camp chair beside the van and turns her face up to the early morning sun. Soon it will be too hot to sit outside, and she will go in and get ready to head to King's Lake to catch up with Bec. With only two weeks to go till Jess's wedding, they need to go over any last-minute details, which will include where to hold the ceremony. She will tell Bec that Lukah is taking her on a reconnaissance to Karijini in the next day or two, and Bec will tease her about her old love.

Girl gossip. It's been a long time since she has indulged in such simple fun, and to her surprise she is looking forward to catching up with her friend.

The catering for the wedding is being taken care of by the local Eco Retreat, and includes "*tantalizing delights made with delicious, traditional bush tucker ingredients*" according to the brochure Bec had given her. A three-piece orchestra is booked and accommodated at the lodge.

She can see it now: simple, elegant, and stunning under a night sky of a million stars. It will be a wedding made for headlines in the national media.

Bec, ever meticulous and with an artist's eye for detail, is catering for the A-List event the same way she organises her son's birthday parties.

They will all be there, the well-connected and influential: monied, high-profile and distinguished. Flying in, their planes lined up in the designated paddocks beside the retreat, alliances formed years ago and cemented by a state government with a nose for well-heeled donors for their next political campaigns.

Corruption, sitting at the tables of an outback retreat, celebrating the marriage of a daughter and a son groomed to carry on the tradition.

Karin has written the story many times in her job as an investigative reporter, but never with her own father as collateral damage. And never where the people involved will do anything to silence the teller of the story.

Her father, who thought he could make his way in a world that locked out people like him. Creator of world-breaking new technology one day; dead the next. Or so the story goes. If there's one thing Karin knows about stories, it's that they can be slanted to suit the teller.

Impatient at the direction of her thoughts, she finishes her coffee and punches out a text.

Meet at King's Lake in ten, before it gets too hot

The response is immediate.

Say please

She pictures Bec, picnic packed and keys in hand, already halfway out the door.

Sorry, please

She is smiling as she pulls on cotton shorts and a sleeveless T-shirt. She adds hiking sandals and runs her fingers through her hair. It takes a couple of minutes to assemble her fold-up bike and attach the dog carrier. "Come on, Trouble. Let's go for a ride."

They hit Happy Valley Road, turn left instead of right, and head for the lake.

King's Lake, the pride of local tourist brochures. In reality, it is a snake-infested dank creek that flows nowhere. A battered No Camping sign is hammered onto a tree, alongside another sign that promises twenty-four-hour video surveillance.

By the time she arrives, Bec is out of the car and sitting at a concrete picnic table shaded by a tin roof.

"You couldn't think of somewhere cooler to meet?"

"And miss a trip down memory lane? No way. We used to come out here and smoke dope." Bec pulls out a thermos and pours iced water into two cups. "Drink up, and next time bring water with you."

Karin picks up a cup and drinks. "We've only come five hundred metres. Remind me again why you live here?" She takes the second cup and pours it into a bowl for Trouble.

Bec refills the cups and slaps Karin's hand as she reaches into the picnic basket. "Wait. I'm not organised."

Karin watches as Bec spreads out a chain-stitched floral tablecloth with matching serviettes. She sets a white plate rimmed with gold in the middle, alongside a bunch of freshly picked frangipanis in a jam jar tied with raffia. She pulls out a Tupperware container and tips a pile of Anzac biscuits onto the plate with a flourish. "Biscuit? Toby helped me make them especially for Aunty Karin."

Karin takes one for her and one for Trouble. "Tell him thanks from us."

Bec grimaces, then tips the container of crumbs on the ground for the dog. "Tell him yourself when you come for a barbecue tonight. I won the meat raffle, and it's tradition that I share the spoils."

"Invitation accepted. What else did I miss last night?"

"You mean the stripper? I'd tell you, but you know the rules."

Karin sighs and snags two more biscuits while Bec is busy unwrapping a plate of watermelon. "What happens at the party, stays at the party, right? Pity."

"But what happened between you and the handsome policeman after you left is fair game. Tell me everything."

"Nice try, but no banana. Tell me about that cute kid of yours instead. What's he going to do when he finishes school?"

"What do you reckon?"

"If he wants to go to uni, he can come stay with me and Trouble in the city."

Bec laughs. "I was indiscriminate with my choice of male companions back in the day. I chose 'em for their looks, not their brains. Poor Toby hasn't got the smarts for university. But he's a good worker. He'll get a traineeship as a diesel mechanic or something with the mines, and stay here like the rest of us."

Karin eyes her friend curiously. "Have you ever wanted to get out? Do something different?"

"Me and Toby are happy enough here." She passes Karin the plate of watermelon. "We're not complaining."

"Your art is hanging in Parliament House. You could open a gallery in the city. Make a name for yourself."

"What would I do in the city? You can't hear yourself think in those places. Besides, my inspiration is out here, in the wide open spaces of the outback. What can I say? I'm a simple girl with simple pleasures."

"Lukah says you and Arno have linked up."

"We have, and before you ask, we're not getting married. We like things the way they are. Can we talk about the actual wedding now, please?" She places a ring binder on the table. "We've got official bridesmaid work to do."

Karin reaches for a triangle sandwich. "I officially declare this bridesmaid meeting open. Now, tell me everything you've done while I listen and nod."

It is as Karin suspected. There is nothing for her to do that Bec hasn't already thought of. "I'm lucky you're letting me choose the spot for the ceremony."

"I figured it wouldn't matter where you chose. It's all magic out there. Just don't forget to organise buses to get everyone from the resort and back again. Lots of iced water in eskies for the trip out. Champagne for the ride back." She makes a note in her file. "And don't forget drone permissions for the media."

"I VISITED THE CEMETERY this morning," Karin says as Bec closes the folder and helps herself to a chocolate rum ball. "Someone's been tending Dad's grave. The plastic flowers were fresh."

Bec's gaze narrows. "I don't know why you bothered to visit the bastard. He never did you guys any good."

"It's been a long time," Karin says. "I've decided that indifference is better than anger. Besides, I'm curious about what really happened to him. I never asked, and nobody ever told me anything, other than it was a tragic accident and all that."

"Would you have listened? You were pretty full of yourself back then."

"I was, wasn't I?" Karin looks around her, at the date palms, the mown parklands, the "lake" with its snake-infested reeds. She remembers how they used to ride their bikes out here and camp, back when there weren't rules and threats of surveillance. "Lukah and I shared our first kiss out here."

"And your first joint."

Karin turns back to her friend. "Supplied by you, if I remember correctly."

"What can I say? I had connections. Still do, if you're interested."

"I'm not sure the local law enforcement would approve."

"Oh, yeah, I forgot. Damn. I liked being young better."

"Oh, for the good old days."

"They were good days for the most part, weren't they?"

"We were sixteen and invincible."

"I have a fifteen-year-old son to prove at least one of us wasn't," Bec says with a grin. "But, hey, he was the best thing that ever happened to me, corny as it sounds."

Karin's gaze turns serious. "I'm sorry I wasn't there for you, Bec. Having to pack up and move to the city sucked."

"I felt sorry for you," Bec says with a shrug. "I had my folks and, later, my art. You lost your father and got dragged off to the city."

"Your father—did he ever say anything about Dad's accident?" Karin thinks of Bec's father standing beside her own in the photo in the mining office reception. The two men had their arms slung around each other's shoulders, both looking at the camera like they owned the world.

"Not really—only that Mr Maskell made things right for you all once your Dad was gone. Whatever that means."

Karin wonders. Could it have been Jess's father who gave her mother the money? He'd been the CEO of the mine at the time. And he had been the one who spoke at the funeral. Karin didn't remember much about what he said. Hadn't wanted to listen. She was too angry—at leaving her best friends, the home she'd grown up in, and the love of her life. Lukah was right. She had been angry at the world, and looking for answers hadn't been on her list. But the adults around them must have known. Had they said things to her mother that they couldn't say to a sixteen-year-old girl who hadn't stopped crying for weeks?

"Everyone said it was an accident," Karin says, thinking about old Nev's words at the mine site the day before. "But what if it wasn't?"

"Why would anyone want to kill your Dad?" Bec frowns. "The funeral was brimming over with people paying their respects. I remember that much. They wouldn't do that if he was a bastard, would they?"

Karin picks up a piece of watermelon. "Someone was watching me when I went to the cemetery yesterday. They were in one of the dongas where all the big machinery is kept."

"Maybe they were perving at your arse. Blokes are like that around here—have you forgotten?"

Karin tells her about old Nev and his warning. "He said Dad had a falling out with his mates over his research into automating the trains for the company."

"I heard that story, too. Putting his mates out of work, Dad said. But it was all a long time ago. Why are you asking questions now?"

Karin hesitates. "Mum got a payout of thirty million."

"You're joking." Bec leans forward, her gaze earnest. "It sucks that you lost your father and all that. But your Mum should be living like a queen—"

"Instead of burying herself away in a nothing suburb in the city." Karin smiles sadly. That's what I think too."

"Have you asked her?"

"We don't talk about it. There's a picture of Dad on the mantelpiece and that's about it. Besides, what would I say? *Hey Mum, do you think there's any chance Dad's death wasn't an accident? That he might have been murdered?* Not exactly dinner table talk."

Bec looks away and tips the remaining biscuits back into the Tupperware container. "I guess not. But if what you're saying is even remotely true, the rumour mill would have had a field day. There's no way you can keep anything like that a secret round here, even fifteen years after the event."

"Funny how the rumour that Dad got drunk, laid on the tracks, and waited for a train to slice him to pieces is so much easier to believe."

Bec smiles. "It made a good story for us kids. Well, later, after all the sadness had passed." She moves around the table and stands behind Karin, wrapping her arms around her from behind. "I'm glad you're back. It hasn't been the same around here with one of us missing."

Karin leans back into the comfort Bec is offering. "I've missed you guys too."

"If you want my advice, don't open the can of worms. Everyone's moved on. The drama of the automation is behind us and the world hasn't stop spinning."

"And you don't need some city chick spoiling things."

"Something like that. It's peaceful around here. Just the way we like it."

"Even if it's a lie."

"Even then." Bec rests her chin on Karin's head. "Here's what we're going to do. We're going to go out to old man Maskell's next weekend, and we're going to play nice. We say hello to him and Mrs Maskell and take advantage of all that luxury for two whole days. Then we come back to town, and we give Jess the best damn wedding this town has ever seen." She drags Karin to her feet and envelops her in a hug. "And after it's all over, you, my friend, go back to where you came from."

"You don't think I should just come out and ask Jess's father for the truth?"

"Great idea. He'll say, *Yeah, sure, I got your old man killed, and there's nothing you can do about it except to fuck off back where you came from.* So you see, whichever road you take, the result's the same. Only my way is more pleasant and doesn't spoil Jess's big day."

"Fair point," Karin says with a grin. "Although I'd like to think he would be a little more civilised than to direct a profanity at his daughter's matron of honour. After all, he's one of the local squattocracy. He has a reputation to consider."

"And God knows how many acres raking in millions from mining royalties. A self-made man with squintillions of dollars, which you and I are doing our utmost to spend on this fucking wedding."

"Spend his money and make him bleed, huh?"

Bec nods, her eyes sparkling. "Have you got any idea what it costs to hire out a whole resort for a night? Not to mention the no-fly zone, the security team, and the blasted fiddle players in penguin suits."

"The orchestra you're referring to is highly regarded in the city. I'm impressed you managed to book them."

"It was the publicity, darling. When they heard the world's media would be swarming the place, they couldn't resist. I wanted to get a Swiss chocolate wedding cake flown in from Zurich, too, but Jess pooh-poohed the idea. Said she preferred fruit cake. Her mother has already made it."

"It sounds like the fairytale wedding to end all fairytales, doesn't it?"

"Except for a few minor details." Bec finishes packing up the picnic and doesn't quite meet Karin's gaze.

"Are you talking about what you and Jess were so bothered about last night? Spill. Maybe I can help."

"Like you can just waltz back into our lives and save us all."

Karin smiles. "Mean Girl."

"Florence Nightingale," Bec huffs, then spoils it by grinning. "Is this our first fight?"

"It's kind of fun trading insults. Like old times."

"Nah, I've gotten much better now I'm the mother of a teenager."

"You forget I expose dirty secrets for a living."

"Okay, you've got me. Don't say anything to Jess, but apparently her birth certificate has gone missing. It's a bit touch and go whether we can get another one organised in time. But like I told Jess last night, everything will work out. What's the point of the Maskell name if you can't use it to pull a few strings? Jess is going to speak to her Dad and see if he can expedite things."

The Maskell name. Karin wonders what it must have been like growing up in the shadow of such expectation. "Lukah says she and Grayson are happy, and even if the marriage is about joining two dynasties, underneath all the hype they really do love each other."

"You'll find out for yourself tonight. I've invited the whole gang to the barbecue. And that includes your mutt, or Toby will never forgive me. He's been begging for a dog forever and yours is the closest he's going to get to owning one under my roof."

Karin's gaze turns serious. "You've made good, Bec. Someone to love, something to do and all that."

"I've got my family, a good bloke and an easy life. Don't spoil it for me with that too-smart brain of yours. Spend your mother's millions if she doesn't want to spend 'em. Or better yet, marry Lukah and have his babies and stay here with us. Now there's an idea."

"You've got weddingitis, my friend. Any chance of one more biscuit for my offsider before we head back to camp for a swim? You could join us."

Bec declines her offer with a wink. "Nah. The strip show last night was a doozy, and I need to take the edge off my horny with my man coming off nightshift before you lot rock up."

"Too much information." Karin clips her bike helmet on and lifts the dog into his carrier. "Me and Trouble will head over when it cools down. Text me if you want us to pick up anything at the supermarket."

"Bring your swimmers. We've put a pool in and a deck out the back. You can hold hands with the local copper without the prying eyes of half the town craning their necks to watch."

Karin smiles as she watches her friend drive away. She wishes life could be as simple as dining with friends on a Saturday night with a barbecue, a slab of beer and a swim in a backyard pool. Bec is living the dream, and Karin is envious. She wishes it was enough for her, too. But it isn't. There are too many unanswered questions about her father's death, and too many people unwilling to answer them.

Maybe Bec is right. Dragging up the past is futile. What exactly is she hoping to achieve by revisiting something she has spent years trying to forget. They've all moved on with their lives and Karin coming back and asking questions will only upset people. Visiting her father's grave should be enough. She has said what she needs to say to the man who told her she was a princess then let her down by dying.

Except somehow it doesn't feel like the closure she thought it would. There are too many secrets. Too many lies. And she is trained to get to the truth. A professional, she had told Bec. Only this time the stakes are high and the consequences personal. Whoever killed her father has something to hide that is worth killing for.

And, as Bec said, Karin is poking the tiger.

Chapter 10

A S the temperature creeps past forty degrees, the pool offers blessed relief. Karin feels the dirt and sweat fall away as she strokes up and down its length. Trouble is asleep in the van, aircon blasting, sprawled across the bed, his paws in the air and tummy exposed. At least one of them can enjoy a nap. Karin is restless, and she needs to order her thoughts.

As she counts off a hundred laps, she feels the ache in her muscles relax and her brain begin to re-energise.

What had Bec said this morning? *There's no way you can keep anything like that a secret round here, even fifteen years after the event.* She's right.

She finishes her swim and hauls herself to the edge of the pool, staring briefly up at the mountain that is an ever-changing shadow over the Tourist Park. She grabs her towel, phone and keys, and heads to the shaded gazebo, thankful for the gentle cross-breeze fanning her body.

Not bothering to dry off, she drops into a plastic chair with its coating of red dirt and opens her phone. A quick search and she finds the name she wants.

"Marshall Hennessy, Hennessy Global."

"Hi, Marsh. Karin Baxter from *The Economist*."

"Hey, Kaz. I heard you'd gone rogue."

Karin chuckles. "Don't you love the rumour mill? I've taken a sabbatical. Trouble and I are on a road trip north."

She hears the pause at the other end of the line, as if he is choosing his words carefully. "I heard you'd gone back to your old stomping ground. That you're stirring up the locals."

Trust Marsh not to mess around. "I needed to get away for a while," she says. "Work pressures and all that. It was time to de-stress, so I threw the dog in the van and here we are."

"You chose the town your father was killed to de-stress?" She can hear him tapping his pen. "How's that working out for you?"

"I always planned to come here back one day. To find out what really happened to him."

He sucks in a breath. "So, it's personal. I wondered, when I heard you were off chasing a story."

"You heard I was chasing a story? Isn't that a little odd?"

"Not when it's about the kind of money we're talking about. Your job and mine aren't that different. Six degrees of separation and all that."

"Marsh, you're a hedge fund manager."

"And you're poking the hornets in their nest."

He's right. "Me being back is enough to stir them up. I haven't even started asking questions yet."

Sigh. "What's so important that you're calling me on a Saturday?

"I need some information."

"Of course you do." She pictures him leaning back in his chair. His eyes are closed and he's pinching the bridge of his nose. "You want to buy shares in some mining company in...where did you say you are again? The boondocks?"

"Smart-arse. I'm interested in a technology company, and I don't want to buy shares. I want to know who already owns them."

His chair straightens. "Name?"

"Starr Holdings, the company behind the auto-haul railway in the Pilbara. It's big. Too big to be local."

"You're thinking offshore? International? Whereabouts, exactly?"

"All I know is my father went to America to learn more about the technology. Then he came back home to develop the idea for the iron-ore industry here. It was years in the development stage, longer than expected. Which I'm guessing means more complicated."

"And more money needed than originally estimated. Whoever is behind it would have needed to raise more capital. Did it hit the public arena, do you know?"

"I think it was all hush-hush. It would have caused a huge spike in the mining company's share price if word had gotten out. But it was ten years between my father passing away and any public announcement about the first automated trains running."

"You want me to run a timeline on the tech company's expansion?"

"That would be great. Also, follow up on any asset management submissions, debt redistributions, that kind of thing."

"Am I going to regret helping you?"

"Not for this one," she promises, and crosses her fingers behind her back. "I need you to check through ASIC's records, see if there was any insider trading. Stuff like that."

"Any names in particular I'm looking for?"

"Not that I know of yet. I'll get back to you when I find out more."

"You can't do it yourself because?"

"That's the thing when you take off on sabbatical. They take away your security clearance." She is smiling now. "My shout for lunch next time I'm in town."

"Something tells me that next time may be a while away," he says. "Especially if you're heading north. Tell me what you need to know."

"Background information on the Company. Anything that sticks out. You know the kind of thing."

"So, we're fishing?"

"Maybe. There's one more thing—"

"Does this other thing happen to be related to the first thing?"

"I don't know yet. There was a deposit in my mother's bank account back in '09, after my father died. I was wondering if you could trace it for me."

"You mean break the law?"

"Not exactly. Well. Maybe a little."

"Lucky you're cute."

"And lucky you're happily married, and Ruth is pregnant with your babies."

"Yeah, you've got me there. Which reminds me, this is my weekend off. How soon do you need the information?"

"Whenever you're ready. I'm up here for a couple of weeks for my friend's wedding."

"Interesting. I've heard about that, too. Big merger of two of Western Australia's first families."

"Let me guess. You know about the wedding because you read the gossip columns in your spare time?"

"Nope. This one's been in the wind for a while. When mergers the size of your friend's marriage happen, they can move share prices. I'm merely doing my job by staying abreast of current affairs."

"Tell me neither of the parties are on your books. And that we're not going to end up in jail for breaking client confidentiality."

"We're safe. Our fund is big on transparency and wary of risk. A stellar reputation, if I say so myself. But you already know that, or you wouldn't be coming to me."

"True. It also helps that you're the soul of discretion and that I used to do Pilates with your wife. I've got dirt on you."

"So one of us is not above a little blackmail, and it isn't me."

"You don't want the godmother of your babies involved in criminal activity, do you?"

"I want the godmother of my babies to stay on the right side of the law. And to keep herself safe."

"You know me, Marsh."

"You'd better be. It's one thing to hide behind the anonymity by being a highly respected investigative journalist. But up there, you're back on your home turf. Everyone knows everything about you and will make up what they don't."

"I'm back for my friend's wedding. It's not my fault some people have long memories."

"I must admit you've got me curious. As long as Ruth doesn't go into labour with my babies, I'll do a little digging and get back to you."

"Thanks, Marsh. Appreciate it."

"One last thing. If your mother's sitting on thirty million, why—"

"Don't ask. And I won't have to tell you it's sitting in a passbook account in a shoebox at the bottom of her wardrobe."

"Maybe after we solve the mystery of where the money came from, we can look at putting it to work for your Mum."

"Sounds like a plan. Thanks Marsh, and hi to Ruth for me."

Marsh is a good man, and when she goes back to Perth, she will keep her promise and feed him, and his wife and babies, lunch. She just doesn't know when that will be. Right now, her mind is too scattered to think properly about future Karin. Survival of current Karin is taking up all her energy.

Chapter 11

WHAT on earth did guests take to a barbecue in a mining town where everyone had waist-deep freezers and wine fridges stocked for every occasion?

She scans the supermarket aisles. In front of the checkouts are flowers, cellophane-wrapped and fresh in today. She chooses three bunches, heads to the self-service aisle, and uses her phone wallet to pay. At the bottle-o next door she grabs a bottle of cab sav. Shopping done, she unties Trouble, who is asleep in the shade of a giant sculptured ring-tailed dragon.

"Come on, dog. Let's go party." She shoves the wine into her backpack and slings the pack over her shoulders, grabbing Trouble's leash with the hand not holding the grocery bag full of flowers. She is still wearing her swimsuit from the afternoon—covered by a cotton A-line dress—and her hiking sandals.

Trouble dances ahead of her as they cross the football oval to Bec's house. Karin can't help thinking that her friend has done well for herself as she stands at the gate of the air-conditioned four bedder with a pool.

Before she has time to knock the door is flung open, and Toby charges out. She isn't sure who launches themselves on who, the dog or the boy, but it will be the last anyone sees of the duo for the next little while as they disappear into Toby's room.

Bec calls her inside and takes the flowers. "How did you guess? Lilies, my favourite."

Karin grins. "I was spoilt for choice, sorry."

Arno joins them and greets Karin with a hug. Jess and Grayson are in the pool—which leaves one person missing.

Karin cocks an eyebrow at Bec. "A certain someone couldn't make it, huh?"

"You wish," a hypnotic voice rumbles in her ear, as strong arms wrap around her from behind.

She'd recognise those hands anywhere. The thought of them on her body kept her awake half the night and—damn him—he knows it.

"Hi Lukah." She steps out of his embrace, rummages in her backpack, and pulls out the wine. "Make yourself useful and chill this for me."

"What's your poison?" Arno asks as he heads to the fridge.

"Anything cold is fine." She props herself on a kitchen stool and watches as Bec throws chopped potatoes into a bowl, followed by yoghurt, herbs, and diced onion.

Arno passes her a bottle in a stubby holder. "Masto's, a local ginger beer from Broome. The stuff will knock your socks off if you down enough of it."

She smiles. "My kind of drink."

As the conversation becomes general, she relaxes. She has missed the easy camaraderie of her friends.

The hand resting lightly on her knee as Lukah comes to sit beside her tells her he is thinking along the same lines.

"Weddings, hey?" Lukah says. "Makes the most hardened of us mellow." He turns to her and grins. "What do you reckon, Baxter? Want to try a little romance with an old friend in the pool?"

Before she can summon an answer, Bec slaps a spatula on the bench. "Cut it out, you pair. There are impressionable young ears listening from the next room." The effect is spoilt as she sends dove eyes to Arno, who is getting the meat out of the fridge.

"Mate," Arno says to Lukah, passing him a bowl of sliced onions and a handful of utensils. "Let's go barbecue. We'll send Jess in to do girl talk and keep Grayson out with us to discuss secret men's business."

Bec rolls her eyes and passes Karin carrots and grater. "He's dirty about the stripper last night and he's planning to even things up at the buck's night."

"Is Grayson the type to do strippers? I thought he'd be more a cigars and high-stakes poker game kind of guy."

"I think the goal is to show him how the other half live. You know, people who work for a living and drink beer out of cans."

"Poor Grayson."

"Poor Jess, you mean. She'll have to start hosting soirees and book her kids into boarding schools before they're born."

Karin stops grating. "Getting an invitation to a Maskell event really means something, huh? Lucky we've got the inside run with Jess. Who would have thought smearing our faces with Nutella sandwiches together when we were in Prep would see us hobnobbing with the rich and famous crowd?"

"I've always wondered why Jess didn't do the boarding school thing and slummed it with us instead."

"Maybe Mrs Maskell was the precursor of the helicopter parent and couldn't bear to be parted from her princess daughter. She was always around when we were kids, remember?" Karin pushes back her stool and moves to the fridge. "She attended every sports carnival, swimming race and tennis social."

Bec opens an overhead cupboard and pulls out three champagne glasses. "Overprotective."

"Too obsessed with her daughter to send her away to school." Karin pulls a bottle of Veuve Clicquot from the fridge, holds it aloft like a prize, and opens it with a pop.

"Now that's a sound I like," a new voice chimes in. Jess plonks herself down on the stool beside Karin. "Glad to see my bridesmaids are on the job."

Bec places the glasses on the bench. "While you get it on in the pool with a strange man in gold-crested boxers."

"My future husband happens to look cute in boxers." Jess snags a glass and holds it out to Karin. "And even cuter out of them."

"Skite." Bec picks up a glass and shoves it in front of Jess's.

Jess pulls Bec's arm down and moves her own glass closer to the bottle. "Jealous."

Karin points to the bench. "Play nice, children." And waits while they place their glasses in front of her. Bec nudges hers forward an inch. She wags a finger at her friend, fills all three glasses and places the bottle in a silver ice bucket. "Cheers to the bride."

"And the best bridesmaids a girl could wish for."

"About that." Karin's face is innocent as she leans her elbows on the bench. "Bec and I were thinking red bridesmaids' dresses. Bright flaming red. With matching nail polish and lipstick."

Jess cocks her head to one side and studies them. "Would look good against the backdrop of the gorge," she muses. "Yep, the optics work for me."

"Ah, but will your mother approve?" Bec asks, poker-faced. "Without the Julia Maskell seal, we're cooked."

"Leave my darling mama to me, children. Better, let's corner her together next weekend at the station dinner and go over everything. You're both coming, aren't you?"

"Wouldn't miss it," the bridesmaids say in unison.

"Good. Things are getting a tad crazy out there, and I could do with a bit of moral support. I've never seen her so on edge. Even Dad is keeping his distance from her, and he's the one to blame for this whole big wedding thing in the first place. He introduced me to Grayson, joked he was going to be his father-in-law one day, and now look at the pickle we're in."

"You let your father choose your future husband?"

"What can I say? My father has good taste. I had to get married eventually, he said, and voila, a handsome hero flies in with his private plane and sweeps me off my feet. I didn't even have to go looking. It's Mum who's pissed. God knows who she would have chosen for me. I don't think anyone would have ever been good enough, and I'd have been stuck an old spinster forever."

"Poor little rich girl." Bec refills their glasses. "More toasts, this time to rich husbands with private planes. All I got was a mine worker who does night shift and drops filthy overalls on the laundry floor on the way to bed at six o'clock in the morning."

"At least you pair have men." Karin sips her champagne and looks forlorn. "All I've got is a damn dog."

"Err...I'm not sure a certain policeman would agree with you on that." Bec is looking over Karin's shoulder and, too late, Karin feels herself hoisted off her chair and locked against a familiar chest.

"Sorry, ladies. Mind if I steal this woman away? She promised me a swim in the deep end."

"Put me down," Karin mutters as Bec snatches the champagne glass out of her hand. "I don't want to swim."

"Liar." Lukah strides out onto the back deck and drops into the pool, still holding her in his arms.

Before she can splutter a retort, he wades towards the deep end of the pool away from the lights of the deck and ducks them both underwater, stealing her breath with a fast kiss.

"Not fair," she splutters as they surface.

"What, you wanted to stay under the water longer?"

Before she can reply, he pulls her under again. This time the kiss is slower. His hands cradle her face and, somehow, her hands splay across his chest. In her mind, they break the surface all too soon.

"Sorry, I couldn't wait another minute. You're just too damn delectable and I needed to taste you to remind myself you're finally here. With me."

Karin looks around her. She has missed this. Her friends, the laughter, Lukah.

"I've missed you, and never even realised. I'm sorry. I was so determined to block this place out of my life, I blocked the good bits, too."

"I'll take being a good bit." He kisses her again, more slowly this time. "As long as you don't leave again without saying goodbye. I waited for you to swing by that day. The day you left. But you never came."

"I couldn't. Not then. Not later. I had to make a clean break, or I would have broken."

"I know. I understand. But coming back? Is the same thing going to happen again? The Karin Baxter I knew would never have left without saying goodbye. I knew it was the grief that made you go. But later, you still didn't call. Until finally I had to admit you weren't coming back. Except you're here now. Are you going to kiss and run again, chica? Because now would be a really good time to tell me. Before we...you know, take this any further."

"A lot has changed in fifteen years. I've changed. We've changed. And there are things I need to do..."

"That a policeman can't know about? I already figured out that much. But you can trust me, sweetheart. Trust me to keep you safe while you look for whatever it is you're looking for. I've never given up on us, even if you have. And I'll be waiting when this is all over, whatever it is, and then maybe we can revive a few of those memories."

Karin wraps her arms around his neck and presses against him. "I like that idea," she says, burying her face in his neck. "I like that idea a lot."

"Hey, you lovebirds, cut out the dirty talk. I'm calling Toby and Trouble out. Clean up your act, pronto." Arno is standing at the head of the pool. He glares at them in the darkness, then spoils it with a wink.

Karin pulls away, but keeps her hands linked around Lukah's neck. "I do trust you," she says softly. "But this is something I have to do on my own."

She pulls his head down and presses her lips against his, making a promise with her body even though she is not yet ready to say the words. Then she pushes away and swims to the shallow end of the pool, where her dog is barking excitedly and Toby is about to bomb her and mess up what's left of her dignity. She laughs and grabs the boy and tugs him under the water.

For a few hours, she will let herself relax and be with her friends. Time enough later for other things.

Chapter 12

"**S**OMETHING tells me we're not going back to my place so I can rock your socks off."

She grins at Lukah in the dark. "I didn't ask you to walk me home."

"And disappoint our matchmaking friends? Face it, darling—they all think we're a couple, and that we're off to do what couples do."

"That would explain why Bec offered to keep Trouble overnight. Here I was thinking it was for Toby's sake."

"Nah. They're rooting for us—so to speak."

She stumbles and he strikes an arm out to steady her. "Where are we going anyway? This isn't the way to the Tourist Park."

Her mind is still on Lukah's wording, but she rallies, commanding her thoughts back to the topic at hand. "I want to know if it's possible to stop an ore train by waving the colour red, or whether it's just a myth."

He groans. "Why don't you ask at the Information Centre like a normal tourist?"

"Because seeing is believing." He can make what he wants of her words. She does not owe him an explanation.

Lukah places his hands on her shoulders and waits for her to meet his gaze. "How exactly does someone go about stopping a train two kilometres long and weighing thirty-five thousand tonnes?"

She shrugs. "We tell it to." She has read that the train her father was driving the night he died was a 7707 made up of two locomotives and a driver at the front, followed by a hundred and thirty wagons, then two remote locos and another hundred and thirty wagons, with an electronically controlled braking system. A problem occurred when communication broke down between the front and remote locos, and the electronic braking system engaged to stop the train. Her goal tonight is to see if she can replicate the breakdown. But first she needs to stop the train.

"Dad would have confirmed with train control that there was a problem when the automatic brakes system kicked in and then stepped off the train to manually apply hand brakes so that it didn't roll. But something went wrong, and the wagons rolled forward. With my father under the wheels."

"That could have been an accident, like they said."

"Maybe. The report says *death by misadventure*, and risk assessments were upgraded to prevent accidents like that from happening again. They blamed driver fatigue, seven-day rosters, and lack of driver training on the new braking system."

"But your father wasn't just a bloke on roster."

"No. He was meticulously recording stoppages to justify automating the system. A breakdown would have worked against him."

"And favoured those with a vested interest in keeping their jobs."

"Maybe they were trying to scare him and something went wrong."

"Maybe. And maybe they're still around, and they'll do anything to stop the truth getting out."

"It's been fifteen years. I want to check the facts, that's all?"

As if he can read her mind, he reaches for her hand. "I'm guessing you've got a plan on how this is going to go down."

"Sort of. A train the weight and length Dad was driving takes a kilometre to stop. His train came to a stop here at the overpass. Which meant the communication breakdown happened out around Mt Nameless. Between the mountain and here, people would have been working, even in the middle of the night. People would have seen and heard and come to investigate. People who may not have been interviewed at the time."

"We're going to stop a train and see who turns up?"

"Unless you've got a better idea."

"My idea was to take you home to bed, chica. Not get us killed."

"I have no desire to die tonight either. Our job is to wave a red light, make a train screech to a halt, and watch who comes to investigate."

"You know, this could have been kind of romantic," he says. "If it wasn't so fucking dangerous. Flushing out a murderer kind of kills the mood."

She picks up the pace. "Come on. I don't know what time the train is coming, and I don't want to miss it."

"Again, if you had asked me—"

She stops and turns to him. "You know the train times?"

"Everybody does. Mothers put their babies to bed by the trains and Daddies get out of bed in the morning to the same sound. The things run like clockwork. What's your plan? If—by some stroke of luck—we do manage to stop the train, what happens? It's not as if there will be a train driver that we can ask to borrow a match to light a cigarette."

Karin grins. "What do you take me for? You think I'd be silly enough to get caught?"

Lukah slaps his forehead. "The overpass. Fuck no. You not really going to—"

"No," she replies. "I'm not. We are."

She starts walking again, this time more quickly, as she swings the pack around to her front and rummages inside. She pulls out the torch. "Which one of us is going to climb up there, you or me?"

"Why do I have the feeling that I already know the answer to that one?" Reluctantly, Lukah takes the torch.

"Ever the gentleman," she says, then turns serious. "Remember, once you wave the torch and the train stops, run. There will be people everywhere."

"What will you be doing? Or don't I want to know?"

"I'll be down on the tracks, watching and waiting."

"On second thoughts, you climb up and do the torch waving, and I'll keep an eye out. That way I'll know you're safe."

"Lukah," she says. "It will be less obvious if the local copper is seen out and about. I'll be discreet, promise."

Lukah rolls back on his heels. "You're not telling me everything, are you?"

"Not everything, no." She does not elaborate.

He searches her face. "Risky."

"The best stories always are. Trust me, I've been in this situation before. Nobody will be paying any attention to me. All eyes will be on the train."

"You hope." He takes the torch and starts to climb up the bank to the overpass. She waits until he disappears, crouched down low so that anyone watching from the mine site can't see him.

She skirts the path and heads for the mine's office she and Trouble had visited the other day. Out in the open there is nowhere for her to hide—and if anyone sees her, she's screwed. She feels the earth's rumble as the train begins its pass through the town. Lukah will do his thing with the train and hopefully it will stop. Workers will come running. And she will use the disruption to break into the office.

The train noise gets louder until it is deafening. The screeching of brakes. The long, lumbering slowing of the train as two hundred and fifty wagons come to a grinding halt. Men appear with torches. Work utes with flashing lights race parallel to the train line.

Karin waits. She pushes the office door, and it swings open easily. So much for security.

She doesn't risk turning on a light. From memory, there should be a door off to the left, which she assumes it is the mine manager's office. She opens it and, after making sure all the blinds are closed, turns on her phone torch. She heads to the filing cabinet cabinets and begins to rummage. Thanks to Marshall, she has an idea of what she is looking for. Contracts, signatures, all on letterheads, traceable evidence back to the source. Follow the money. She raises her phone and takes photos of what she needs.

There is one more thing before she leaves. She scans the walls till she comes to the photograph over the receptionist's desk. She lifts her phone and clicks off a shot of the men standing tall and proud with her father.

One of those men had betrayed him and gotten him killed.

And she intends to find out who.

Her father, crumpled across a railway line.

She closes the door and slips into the shadows as men start filing back to the mine site. The train fires up and begins to pick up speed.

At that moment the moon comes out from behind the clouds. She looks up at Mt Nameless and vows that the man who killed her father will pay.

The next step in her plan requires that she is more careful. Stopping a train is one thing. Confronting a man who has hidden his crime for fifteen years is another level of dangerous altogether.

Chapter 13

SHE takes a shortcut across the railway lines and follows their contours towards Happy Valley Road. With all the commotion, there is nobody to tell her she is trespassing. She reaches into her backpack for her phone, and has just shot off a text to Lukah when she hears the crunch of tyres on the rocky ground in front of her.

A vehicle appears from the shadows, its headlights turned off. The revs of the diesel engine are low, like it has been idling, biding its time. It is the old bloke, Nev, and he is hidden from the mine by the railway workshops that run beside the tracks for almost a kilometre.

He pulls the vehicle to a halt beside her. "Hop in."

Karin meets his gaze with an unflinching bravado she doesn't feel. "I don't think so."

"Darlin', yer out in the middle of nowhere. If I wanted to do yer harm, we wouldn't be talkin' about it first."

She nods. "Fair point."

She places her hand on the doorhandle and yanks it open, the noise grating in the silence. She pushes a hard hat and goggles onto the floor of the cab, and they land next to a pair of orange rolled up overalls slung through the handles of an Esky.

Karin climbs into the vehicle, the shadows of workshops enveloping them in darkness. In front of her Mt Nameless is backdropped by a carpet of stars so thick they almost crowd out the sky. She remembers to breathe.

The old man winds down the window and spits a golly. "What you did tonight was fuckin' stupid. Anyone could 'a seen yer. And probably did, for all yer know."

In, out. "I had my reasons."

"They'd wanna be good ones. Word's out that yer sniffin' around askin' questions. Draggin' yer copper mate along is askin' fer trouble."

Karin knows bringing Lukah was a mistake. The night with her old friends had clouded her judgement. Her rule in the city had always been to keep her professional and personal lives separate. Investigating her father's death crossed the line between the two. The old man's warning is a timely reminder.

"You're right," she says softly. "I'll be more careful next time." What she doesn't say is that she will stop asking questions.

The look he gives her tells her he notices. "It's on yer head. Don't say I didn't warn ya."

"Is that what this is, a warning?"

"Call it what yer want. Jes' don't be stubborn like yer old man over stuff ya know nothin' about."

First her uncle, and now her father's old mate warning her. It could be a coincidence, but Karin doubts it.

"You don't think my father's death was an accident either, do you?"

"Yer the big-shot reporter. You tell me." He rummages in the console between them and pulls out an envelope. It is stained with grease and dirt and has clearly been there for some time. "'Ere, this is for you. Try not to let anyone know I gave it to ya."

She glances down at the envelope, not yet ready to commit to taking it. "You picked an interesting place to give me whatever it is in there."

He meets her gaze with a grin that holds no mirth. "I value me own hide. If anyone sees me talkin' to the traitor's kid, I'd be done in just like 'im."

"The official account is it was a work accident."

"There was an official version, and there was what folks were sayin'."

Her uncle, too, had mentioned the rumours going around at the time. Like they were some kind of male code—like killing her father for his betrayal was acceptable payback. It all sounded very neat. Convenient, even. If someone wanted to cover a murder, blaming his mates made sense. Rough justice in a mining town was rarely questioned back in the day, and even more rarely investigated.

Karin is starting to believe the rumours were a smokescreen, and that the man beside her thinks so, too. "Were you there the night he was killed?"

"I was on shift, yeah. But so was a lot of other blokes."

"They would have talked about what they saw. You must have heard what they were saying."

"Officially, we was told to keep our traps shut."

"And unofficially?"

"I dunno. After Big Jim went under the wheels, the site was closed and we were sent 'ome. I didn't feel much like goin' to the pub to listen to blokes bullshit on about what might or might not have 'appened."

Karin frowns, picturing the scene. Her father dead on the tracks, his mates standing around not knowing what to do. She closes her eyes, forcing all emotion from her mind. Think. Someone must have taken charge. Cleaned up the mess. Ordered the men not to talk to the media.

It would not have been hard. The local newspaper was run out of Karratha four hours away, and there would have been no television crew within cooee. No social media back in those days. That left the mining company to release a statement. The matter was closed, except for an official investigation that would take years. No wonder the rumour mill kicked into overdrive.

"You were there, yet you didn't believe the official version of my father's death?"

He shoves the filthy envelope towards her. "I know what I saw, and things didn't add up."

The envelope is slit open at the top. Inside is a black USB. "What's on it?"

"Just stuff. Dunno if any of it'll help, but it's there if you can make head or tail of it."

She takes the stick out of the envelope and pockets it. "Why now? Why me?"

It is Nev's turn to stare straight ahead, like he is looking to the mountain for an answer. "Your old man got caught up in things he didn't understand. 'E wasn't a criminal. Just stupid."

The silence sits between them. Karin waits while he gathers his thoughts. It is a trick she learnt years ago. People feel the need to fill a silence. Not so the old man. Silence hangs over him like a cloak.

"You never gave up," she says finally. "All this time and you still believe in him."

He turns and looks at her. "An' maybe I'm wastin' me time talking to ya."

Is he? She was sixteen when her father died—a hormone-riddled teenager who got angry when Daddy didn't come home from work one night, upsetting the pattern of her life. She blamed her father, took her anger out on her mother, and cried herself to sleep for months.

And now, a crazy old man is offering her his version of what happened on a memory stick. And wondering if she knows what to do with it.

He is wrong.

"Neville Schulz, sixty-three years old," she recites, using the tone she used with all her interviewees, meant to disarm yet prove her credentials at the same time. 'You came out from Liverpool, England, wet behind the ears, and got a job with Pilbara Rail. You were a union man through and through, a rabble-rouser who caused a whole lot of mischief in your day. But you've gone quiet. People say you've lost your mojo and they leave you alone to see out your days. Some wonder why you didn't leave after my father died. Thought you had something to do with it and that it would have been prudent for you to get out of town."

His nod is barely discernible, his fists tight on the steering wheel. "While they're watchin' me, they're leaving others alone."

Karin reaches for the doorhandle. It has been a long day and an even longer night, and she has had enough of the crazy old man with his secrets.

"Wait." He pulls out a battered silver tin, opens the lid, and takes out a small sheath of white paper and a pinch of tobacco. She watches as he rolls a cigarette and strikes a match. He lights up, and she sees his face. The pain is there for her to read, as if her father's death was yesterday. He hasn't forgotten. Nor has he forgiven. He has been biding his time.

"You've been tending his grave, haven't you?"

"Meybe."

"The inscription—was that you?"

His eyes crinkle at the corners. "Meybe." He sucks on his cigarette and exhales. "There's only three things that matter in this world." Karin waits while he puffs on his cigarette before he continues. "Land, money, and power." His gaze locks on hers. "Ya can't have any of them without the others, and if you do, you lose 'em all real quick. That was yer old man's mistake. He had the land and he got the money. But the third one, that third one—it was tricky. Too tricky in the end."

She cocks her head. The inscription on her father's grave suddenly makes sense. *Hold your friends close, and your enemies closer.* She drops her hand to her knee and relaxes back into the bucket seat. "They say it's not what you know," she murmurs, "but who you know."

Nev finishes his cigarette and tosses the butt out the window. She waits, instinct telling her he is not yet done with his story.

"In the early days this was cowboy country. Take what you want. Disappear with the winnin's. By the time yer old man came along, things had changed. There were gatekeepers. And they had the controllin' hand. Yer old man didn't like it." He pauses, and she makes no effort to fill the void. She is not even sure she wants him to continue.

The truth of what he is about to say already sits like lead in her stomach. "Find who yer old man was dealin' with and you've got yer killer."

That word again. Nev confirms what she has always known in her heart. Someone killed her father. In cold blood. She barely registers that he is still talking.

"Go back a way. Do yer homework. See who is still standin' and why. You've got connections. Use 'em. And remember, you never got that thing in your pocket from me." He screws up the envelope and tosses it out the window after his cigarette butt.

This time, Karin opens the door and scrambles out—as if by distancing herself she can shut out his words. *Who was in charge? Follow the money. They killed your old man and split the profits.* Like a child throwing a tantrum, she wants to cover her ears and block out his words. *Land, money, and power.* It is like every story she has ever written. Only this time it is her family's story, and she is not sure how it will end. Following the money sounded well and good in the cold light of day, but in the dark of night, it feels like she will vomit where she is standing.

As if he can read her mind, Nev calls to her as he winds up his window. "Take care walking home, darlin'. Yer wouldn't be the first to disappear out 'ere in the dark." A soft laugh follows his words, and he is gone.

She listens as the sound of his vehicle fades away. Good guy or not, he intended to frighten her, and he succeeded. Instinctively she scoops up the discarded envelope and shoves it in her pocket with the USB. Her fingers curl around the memory stick. She is in control, she reminds herself. It is her job, and she is good at it.

It is no coincidence that Nev was waiting for her tonight. Whatever information the old man has given her it is too dangerous for him to act on himself. He is taunting her. Is she good enough to track down the person who killed her father, or is she all piss and bravado?

She forces her attention to the problem of finding her way back to the tourist park. And to the computer screen that will give her the answer to the old man's question.

Chapter 14

BACK at the van she grabs a towel, toiletries, and pyjamas and heads to the shower block. There is a light on the corner of the building, and a myriad of flying ants swarm her face as she opens the steel grilled door of the ladies and hurries inside. The shower block lights up automatically on her entry.

She chooses a shower cubicle at the end of the row and hangs her towel on the hook. The sound of crickets keeps her company while she showers. The night is still and hot, and she stands under the cold water for longer than she should before turning it off and towelling herself dry. It is quiet without the running water to distract her. Too quiet. She misses her dog. Without Trouble to keep her company she is too alone. *Disappear without a trace.* She pulls her dressing gown tight and hurries back to the van.

She checks her phone, but there is no message from Lukah. She hates that she has checked. She is a grown woman. Able to take care of herself.

Retrieving the USB from the pocket of her dress, she dumps the dirty clothes in the washing basket. She sits at the fold-out table, opens her laptop and plugs in an adapter to accommodate Nev's low-tech storage device.

She sips from her water bottle as dozens of files fill the screen. The files are unnamed, but they are in date order and go back way past when her father was killed. She scrolls to the earliest date, June 1993, and opens the file. It contains a single photograph.

Her fingers pause on the keyboard, part of her wanting to close her computer and go to bed.

Pretend she has not seen her parents smiling back at her.

She cannot look away.

She closes her eyes briefly, then forces herself to study the image, because it is not just her parents she recognises. Three couples stand side by side, and a man standing on his own at one end. Their dress is formal, the women in floor-length dresses and the men in suits with crisp white shirts and bowties. The image is uncaptioned.

There is another file dated the same month and it, too, contains an image, this time of the four men. They are standing together, their arms thrown over each other's shoulders, laughing at the camera like someone has told them to say *sex* and captured the image as they shout the word. It is captioned *Graduation, University of Western Australia, 1989.*

The next file is dated 2006—but it is the two older files with the thirty-year-old photographs that hold her attention.

Her heart is beating faster than it should be, and her hands shake slightly as she opens the images side by side on the screen. Group of men on the left, couples on the right.

She zooms in on the faces of the first couple. Her parents are younger. Happier. Closer than they were when she was growing up. She has never seen this photo in the boxes her mother keeps in the bottom of her wardrobe.

She scans the other faces, recognizing Julia and Roland Maskell, but she does not know the third couple or the man standing on his own.

She zooms out and scans her mother's dress. It is floor-length, scooped at the neck, and falls to the ground in soft baby-blue folds. Simple, elegant, and flattering. Her mother's hair falls loosely to her shoulders. Karin reaches out a finger, as if she can stroke the pale blond strands.

Her mother looks pretty as she gazes at the camera. Her eyes are wide and innocent, and her fingers are entwined with those of her husband, who stands tall and handsome at her side, in a suit that fits his broad shoulders like it is tailor made.

Karin cannot recall ever seeing her father in a suit. Nor can she remember her parents ever holding hands. Her parents being young and in love is not something Karin has ever considered. It is not how children see their parents. But the evidence in front of her is irrefutable. What went wrong to change her mother from innocent and in love to the angel-emoji-sending woman at the cemetery?

Was it just the passage of time or had something else happened between her parents to dim the innocent love she sees shining in her mother's eyes on the screen?

She casts a cursory glance over the Maskells. She is less surprised this time. Julia is regal in a gold-specked sheaf, deceptive in its simplicity. Her hair is French-braided and tied in a bun at the back of her head, and a gold ribbon is woven through the braid like a statement. She stares at the camera like she owns it, her poise evident in the tilt of her chin and the unsmiling line of her mouth.

Her husband casts an equally impressive pose in a double-breasted charcoal grey suit and matching bowtie. His hair is flecked with silver, and he is every bit the aristocrat as he looks down at the camera. Born with a spoon in his mouth, as the saying went. The couple do not hold hands, but they are united through the touch of their shoulders.

Karin does not recognise the other two men, although the woman with her body half-draped over one of them and pouting provocatively at the camera is the most intriguing person in the photo. Her head is thrown back, and there's an energy about her that makes the other women pale in her shadow.

She is tall and slim, and the way she is draped over the man in the centre of the photo shows that she is on her best behaviour, but only because she chooses to be. Karin would not be surprised to see her lean up and lick the side of the man's neck like she wants to devour him. She is lithe and sensuous, and she is having fun posing for the photograph, and she looks at the camera as if she is daring it to come closer and look down her cleavage.

The dress she is wearing gives lie to the word *formality*. The maroon velvet clings to her body, from its pencil strap shoulders down the curve of her body to a long split from her thigh to the ground. One bare thigh is pressed across the man, a black garter belt clearly visible, and one of her arms is curved around the back of his head likes she is rubbing him there. She is a cat, and he is her cream.

Karin cannot help thinking she is looking at characters on a stage as she studies the photograph. A play is about to unfold, and her parents are actors. Is this what old Nev wants her to see? Old friends whose stories merge and drift and finally fall apart in full public view?

She sits back and closes her eyes, taking stock of what she has seen. The fact that the four men went to university together in Perth is noteworthy. And they are together again four years later.

A ball perhaps? The four men taking the opportunity to reunite for the first time since their university days? She scans the photograph for details. There is nothing that explains the occasion other than velvet drapes in the background, red carpet underfoot and a cordon of gold chain threaded through poles of the same colour.

Maybe it is a photograph from the social pages of *The West Australian*, the Notable & Newsworthy section. A-Listers pausing to pose for the camera. So recognizable they do not need a caption.

Whatever the reason, it is as outside Karin's experience of her childhood as it can get. She cannot imagine her parents dancing and laughing and drinking champagne. Her childhood memories are of the adults getting together for card nights while Karin had sleepovers with her friends.

She has never considered that her parents had a life outside the Pilbara mining town where she grew up. It is a betrayal of sorts, and she is not sure how she feels about it.

Old Nev had tried warned her. *Follow the money and you'll find out what really happened that night.* He has provided photographs. And more. There are dozens of files for her to go through. But she has had enough for one night. She needs to sleep. Gather her thoughts. Decide what she is going to do next.

She needs to talk to her mother, but is too late to call her now. Tomorrow is soon enough to ask her about the people in the photographs.

And the life she lived before her daughter was born.

Chapter 15

KARIN wakes to the buzz of her phone.

    Upsidaisy, chica. Time to go location scouting.

She rolls onto her side and pulls open the curtain. "You can't be serious," she mutters. Lukah is sitting on a trail bike outside her door, the pre-dawn light hitting the mountain behind him and haloing his face like the archangel of her dreams. She lets the curtain fall back into place, shutting out his smirk. He knows she hates mornings, especially without coffee.

Her phone buzzes again. He has sent through a snap of the open storage box on the back of his bike.

> Coffee to go
> And pastries
> Pack a swimsuit
> Or not 😬

Karin smiles reluctantly and gives in to the inevitable. She crawls off the end of the bed and reaches for the overhead cupboard. Maybe Lukah is right. A day to process the memories the photographs of her parents have stirred is just what she needs. She pulls on shorts and T-shirt, then grabs a black one-piece swimsuit and towel and stuffs them into her backpack. She fills her water bottle from the filter tap over her sink and slips on her hiking boots.

Phone buzz.

Don't forget a hat.

Damn him. She may have closed her mind to the memories of old times, but Lukah's reminder is a hangover from those days where she was giddy with excitement at seeing him and he was the practical one. It's like he has a list in his brain that he ticks off every time he sees her. A policeman is a good choice of career for an over-caring list maker. She snatches her sunhat off its hook, shoves it into her pack, and heads outside, locking the van behind her.

Lukah reaches out and tugs her towards him, dropping a helmet on her head and adjusting the strap under her chin. He kisses the tip of her nose. "Perfect."

She is getting used to the warm flush that heats her body when Lukah is around. "Nice bike."

He is astride a Ducati DesertX, or so the shining decal proclaims. A stark reminder, if she had needed one, that they are no longer teenagers and Lukah is no longer a starry-eyed guy besotted with his girl. The last time they rode together, they were sixteen on a hand-me-down KTM held together with screws and duct tape. The warning signs are adding up that she needs to be careful with this new Lukah—that he may not be easily distracted if things get complicated.

She slides onto the bike, careful not to bump their precious cargo of coffee, and wraps her arms around his middle. She takes a moment to rest her face against his back. He may have upgraded his bike, but he still smells like the Lukah she remembers, all honest sweat and fresh air with a light coating of Pilbara dirt. It looks like it's going to be a day for memories. She needs to be on her guard.

"Comfy?"

She straightens and smiles at him in the mirror, her expression bland. "Yep."

"Hang on tight." He kicks up rocks as he spins the machine around and heads to the entrance.

The sun chooses that moment to cast the first rays of the day onto the mountain. She relaxes as he guides the bike out of the Park and onto the open road that will take them to Karijini.

As the powerful bike eats up the kilometres, she lets her memories flow. She and Lukah have traversed this road many times. With the wind on her bare arms, she eyes the passing landscape like an old friend, one she hasn't seen in a long time, but remembers intimately.

Too soon, they reach the junction of Mt Bruce and the road to the Karijini National Park. Lukah turns the bike towards the gorges formed over millions of years, the early morning light casting a golden hue over the spinifex and mulga scrub.

Lukah pulls over at the entrance, a stone edifice with a map of the park and a machine demanding seventeen dollars from day-visitors. She climbs off the bike and undoes her helmet, but Lukah has his credit card out and pays her fee before she regains her land-legs.

Her stomach rumbles.

Lukah laughs and lifts their coffees from the storage box. Hers is still steaming as he passes it over. "Hi."

She pulls the lid off her coffee and sips. "Ahh." She leans against the bike and turns her face to the sun. "I've missed this."

"What? Mornings?"

"The view. It's been too long."

He stands beside her, his hip pressed lightly against hers. "Did you ever think of me in the city?"

"Not for a moment."

"Me either." But he is smiling.

She straightens. "Do we have time for a swim before we start work?"

"You've got a swimsuit in that backpack?"

She grins and crosses her fingers behind her back. "Nope."

"Then I'm all for it."

Back on the bike, Lukah turns the bike towards Fortescue Falls. It is at the far end of the string of signposted gorges, past the Information Centre shaped like a goanna with its tail in the air, and is home to Fern Pool. The pool is another memory Karin has no trouble conjuring, and she is happy to bypass the other gorges, one of which will be ideal for Jess's wedding service, if it means she and Lukah will have Fern Pool to themselves before the daily influx of tourists.

Lukah brings the bike to a halt in a bitumen carpark and Karin clambers off. She unclips her helmet and looks around. It has changed. There are sailcloths and timber tables, landscaping and a toilet block. It is stunning in the early morning light and will be again at the end of the day.

"Maybe this isn't a bad spot for a three-piece orchestra, a busload of tuxedoed guests and a ceremony broadcast across Australia." He swings his pack onto his back and takes her hand.

Together, they stroll towards the path that will take them down to the gorge. Later in the day it will be humid, but for now the rock is cool against her trailing fingers. The ferns are damp to her touch and it is already five degrees cooler as they descend.

How many times had they done this climb down to the pool as kids, racing to see who could dive off the wooden deck first? It was always a race to the waterfall where they would sit under the cascading water and watch as the nibbler fish nipped at their toes.

Seeing Lukah naked again is something she is looking forward to. Watching his arse in front of her as he takes the stairs two at a time is already heady. She has earned naked.

He hadn't come looking for her last night, but he is here with her now. And they are about to get naked together.

Last night he had been attentive, refusing to hide his desire. And today they are alone, the nomads not yet awake, the tourist coaches yet to arrive. They have the pool to themselves and there are plenty of shadows under the waterfall.

Lukah strips and dives into the water, before turning around and treading water. "Come on, slow poke."

Karin is struggling with the laces of her hiking boots, her haste making her clumsy. "Not fair."

He makes desultory strokes with his hands. "Need any help over there?"

She kicks off her boots and socks. "You offering?"

"Maybe. Although I must say I'm enjoying the view."

She stands and lifts her T-shirt over her head. She is down to her G-string. "I might sit here for a while." She settles more comfortably on the deck and looks at him through half-closed eyes. "Till it warms up."

"Suit yourself." He folds himself inwards and dives under the water, only to appear again at her feet.

He props his elbows on the deck and she is suddenly conscious of her almost-nudity. He is between her and the water. He smiles like he is clever and she is trapped.

Not so easily, my man. She stands and dives neatly over his head. When she surfaces, she breaks into a crawl. She reaches the waterfall and hauls herself onto the ledge, Lukah a couple of strokes behind her.

She makes scissor movements with her legs, splashing water at him. "I win."

He grabs her feet and pulls himself forward till his chin rests on her knees. "The battle or the war, chica?"

With a quick tug, he pulls her off the ledge—and before she can save herself, she goes under. She throws out her arms and wraps them around his neck as they sink. Their lips collide, and she tastes coffee and water and sunshine. Lukah deepens the kiss as they come up for breath, and this time she feels herself pressed against the ledge, the length of his body against her, the chill of the water forgotten as he deepens their kiss.

"Miss me now?"

"I can't even remember your name."

"Let me remind you."

And he takes them on a trip that, despite her words, she has never forgotten. She wraps her legs around his arse, her hands finding their way to his nape. And as they dance the dance of lovers in the early morning warmth, she knows, finally, that she has come home.

The sun is higher in the sky as they paddle back across the pool, Lukah's strokes pacing hers as they reach the deck and the ladder. She climbs out first and stretches out to dry. Lukah joins her, fingers tangled in hers, the sun warm on their bodies.

She closes her eyes and drifts, listening to the sounds of the insects, the rustle of the wind through the ghost gums, the mating call of a wood swallow. Home is a word she hasn't used in a long time, and she lets it sit alongside the peace of this place and the man at her side.

Maybe it is the magic, the sacredness, but here she is safe to let down her guard and ponder the question she has kept hidden for too long. If home is where the heart is, then why has it taken her so long to come back?

Suddenly restless, as if by moving she can shut off her thoughts, she stands and pulls her T-shirt over her head. She busies herself gathering her things and pulling on her boots.

Lukah is watching her through half-closed eyes, his gaze questioning. She looks out over the pool, avoiding him and his nakedness. Especially that. If she isn't careful, she will drag him back into the water and make stupid doe-eyed confessions she is not yet ready to acknowledge, let alone state aloud.

I'm back because my life stopped when I left here. My father was wrong when he said I was a little girl playing in a man's world. Like old Nev is wrong. It's not my gender that is stopping me finding out the truth. It's my cowardice.

She stands and swings her pack onto her back. "I think I heard a tourist bus arrive."

For a moment she wonders if he will let her get away with the lie. "You're right," he says finally, pushing to his feet. "It's time we earned our keep. What are our instructions again? Find the perfect spot for the perfect wedding."

Karin keeps her gaze firmly on the surface of the pool, pretending his nakedness is not reflected there. "Do you think they'll be happy?"

"They seemed happy enough last night." He pulls on his shorts and drops his T-shirt over his head.

"But how do they know? How can anyone know another person, when you only see what they choose to show you?"

He eyes her thoughtfully. "Want to talk about what's really bothering you?"

She hesitates. "I thought you'd wait for me last night. Or at least text me."

"I was busy." His expression darkens. "Watching you accept a lift from a stranger."

"You saw me get into old Nev's truck?"

He moves to stand beside her, looking down at their reflections, knowing she is watching him dress. "I saw my girl get into a vehicle with another bloke, if that's what you're asking."

He reaches out, his fingers entwined with hers, the faint ripple on the surface of the water distorting the gesture. Beside her, his grip is firm, his touch warm. They look like couple in the reflection, but there is something in his tone that alerts her to a problem in their reflected ideal.

She turns to face him. "You were jealous?"

His gaze is sombre. "I didn't think I had a jealous bone in my body. But seeing you getting a car with another man, I wanted to smash his face in, no matter who he was. I didn't know it was old Nev at first."

She lifts her hand and touches her fingers to his cheek. "And I thought I'd left you dangling on the overpass." She drops her hand to her side. "You could have answered my text, at least."

"And said what? Wish I was there?"

"You could have said something after Nev drove off. Like 'Hey, want me to walk you home?' I would have liked that."

"I can't even explain that part myself. You looked sad." He stares across at the waterfall, as if the answer is there, hidden behind the cascade. "I didn't want to add to your worries. So I followed you home, made sure you were safe. Then hoofed it back to my place to get ready for this morning." His tone lightens. He reaches into his pack and brings out two paper bags. "Someone had to pack the picnic."

"Food! Yes." She snatches the bag closest to her and pulls out an Apple Danish, grinning. "My favourite. How did you know?"

His smile is sardonic. "No idea really. It's not as if I know anything about you."

Karin bites into the Danish. "Nev gave me a USB."

Lukah swings his pack onto his back and opens the other paper bag. "Anything interesting on it?"

"Not much, so far." She bites the last of her Danish and makes a show of licking her lips.

Lukah searches her face, and she wonders if she has pastry crumbs on it. "Methinks the lady lies." He swallows his pastry in two mouthfuls and looks across the pool like he has all the time in the world.

She shrugs. "A bunch of files. A couple of old photographs."

"And?"

"It's the photographs," she admits. "I haven't been able to get them out of my head."

His grip tightens. "Is this about your father's accident? Do I want to know?"

She pulls her hand away and turns towards the track that will take them back along the gorge. "They were photographs of my parents," she says softly. "Before I was born."

Lukah stills. "Wait. It makes sense that he would have photographs of your parents. Didn't he say the last time you met that he and your Dad were mates?"

"These aren't those kinds of photographs." She pulls out her phone and opens the photos app. "They're this kind."

Lukah stares down at her phone before turning his gaze back to hers. "And the files?"

"I don't know yet."

Now is the time for her to admit that seeing her parents like they are in the photographs has thrown her. That she is not sure whether she is chasing a story or watching everything she has ever believed about them unravel in front of her.

Lukah is coming to his own conclusions. "Let me guess. Old Nev is not the bad guy we thought he was."

She laughs. "If the look in his eye last night was anything to go by, he wouldn't hesitate to toss me out on the road and run me over."

"So he was angry. And you were more interested in pumping him for information than getting the hell out of there."

"He was lying in wait for me, remember. Besides, I don't think it's me he's angry with."

"And you know this because?"

It is what she has been wondering herself. "He said something that makes me think he knows more than he is letting on."

"Let me guess. He said follow the money."

It is her turn to laugh. "How did you know?"

"That's what they did in the olden days," he says with a wink. "It's in all the old movies."

"Nev is playing gangster now?"

She feels his hand stiffen in hers. "Nev should keep his mouth shut about things he knows nothing about."

"Lukah, you don't do anger. What's wrong?"

"Everyone knows he's batshit crazy. The old bastard will get you killed with his scaremongering." His tone lightens, but she sees the effort it costs in his expression. "I don't want to lose you again."

"What makes you think I'm yours to lose?"

"Chica, you're mine because we fit. If you try to tell me I'm wrong, I'll take you back over to the waterfall and call you a liar—and this time, we'll have an audience."

Karin belatedly hears the sounds she has missed. She has been distracted by Lukah taking their conversation in directions she is not ready to go. And now there are the unmistakable sounds of tourists about to descend on them.

She pushes him away and turns towards the track. "Wedding venues. Let's get to it before the sun hits the yardarm."

She earns herself a hot kiss for her effort. "Aye, Captain. And just so you know, I may have missed you a bit while you were away in the big city doing important stuff."

"Me too," she says softly, letting her gaze drop to his shorts. "But only a certain bit."

He answers by taking the lead and carving a path for her through the throng of tourists.

She settles for perving at his arse as she follows him. If they are quick, they will get in another swim before they head back to town.

And she knows places tourists don't go.

Chapter 16

THE afternoon temperature has hit the mid-forties, and the air-conditioning in the van is cranked up to high. Karin sits cross-legged on the bed, her laptop balanced on her thighs. Trouble is stretched out beside her, chasing rabbits in his sleep.

As she flicks through the files from the USB, she is starting to see a pattern between the mining prospectuses, shipping invoices, ore tonnage calculations, and franking credits on the various shareholder returns old Nev has meticulously saved over the years. One name, sometimes buried, sometimes not, stands out. Damascus Holdings. The lettering on the logo is a deep maroon—a shade Karin recognises.

The photograph. She opens the file on her laptop and presses her mother's number on her phone.

"Hello."

Karin places her on speaker. "Hey, Mum. Is it okay if I send you through a photo? You'll need to put your phone on speaker while you open the file."

She pictures her mother at the Laminex table in the kitchen, a bowl of fruit in the centre. There will be a teapot and sugar bowl, and a Country Roses cup and saucer with a silver teaspoon sitting in front of her. To one side will be a plate with a slice of vanilla cake and a cake fork. Afternoon tea time. Karin cannot remember her mother's routine ever varying. Until today, when Karin sends her photographs she is not expecting.

"Sure." But Karin can tell by her voice that Marlene Baxter is not sure at all—that her daughter is taking liberties, and it makes her nervous.

Karin waits while her mother opens the photo, the silence punctuated by the faint intake of her mother's breath.

"Where did you get this?"

Lying to her mother does not come easily. "I was in the library, looking up old newspapers to put together a slideshow for Jess's hen's night. This came up in a search for the Maskell name. But there are no names or date."

She is not sure why she is protecting old Nev, except that protecting her sources is as instinctive as breathing. It is a code that has been drilled into her from uni. But this is her mother, and she isn't investigating a story. Is she? She is so busy processing that she has just lied to her mother that she almost misses her answer.

"It was 1993. We were attending the annual Mining Institute ball. We went every year. The boys called it their reunion weekend. We would fly down to Perth and stay at the Crown. They were good times." Her mother's voice is wistful, and Karin pictures her as she forks her cake to her mouth but does not eat.

"You know the Maskells, Julia and Roland. Then there's Rose." Her mother hesitates, "And her husband, Brand. The tall one standing on the far right, that's Holden Caddel. Rose's brother."

"You look really pretty, and Dad's wearing a tuxedo. It must have been special."

"We were young. We drank the best champagne and celebrated like life was an adventure to be conquered. The men were like brothers. When Roland talked about the ore slump and future opportunities, everyone agreed to come up to the Pilbara and check it out. Holden was back from America. And Rose and Brand were up for anything. We flew home in Roland's plane, all of us. It was like an extension of the party."

"Rose? I don't think I've ever heard you mention her."

"Her full name was Damascus Rose." Her mother's voice is so soft that Karin takes the phone off speaker and lifts it to her ear. "All the fellas were besotted with her. Half the women, too."

Karin hears the rattle of crockery, like her mother is settling her teacup with shaky hands. She will dab her mouth with her napkin and touch her hand to her hair. Karin sees the mannerisms for what they are and wonders why she has never noticed before.

Her mother is an expert at buying time.

She is not vague. She is careful.

"We never met anyone like her," she continues. "We all started painting our nails and curling our hair with curling wands. She made us feel sexy and alive in a place where men took sex for granted. We adored her as much as they did—"

Karin's mind is busy joining the dots. Damascus Rose and Damascus Holdings. It can't be a coincidence.

"—but the men were at work all the time and Rose wasn't the type to sit around. The men were out as usual, and Rose... Well, Rose said, 'Why should the men have all the fun?' We packed up and climbed the mountain to watch the sunset. We drank Vermouth and lemonade."

Karin is silent. She has never seen her mother drink. Can't imagine her watching a sunset with her friends.

"There...there was an accident. Rose... She fell. One minute she was standing in front of us, taking a bow over one of her performances...and the next, she was gone. We tried to save her. But it was too late."

Karin is shocked to silence.

"The men concluded their business, whatever it was, and Holden and Brand flew out. We never attended another ball, and there were no more reunions. Not for fifteen years."

Her mother's silence is more telling than any words. A group of friends, and then nothing for fifteen years.

"Jim was working on a new technology to automate the trains. The men decided form a company, raise the necessary capital, and split the profits."

"Damascus Holdings?"

"We talked. Decided it was fitting. That Rose would have liked the big idea of a technology that encompassed the whole Pilbara."

"Only Dad wasn't around to celebrate. But you got your share of the profit anyway. That's what is in the bank book at the bottom of your wardrobe."

"Yes. Why are you dredging all that old stuff up now?"

"I'm not dredging up anything, Mum. It found me. Does this have anything to do with what happened the night Dad died?"

"No."

Karin waits.

"At least, I don't think it does. Bernie just said there was an accident at the mine and that Jim had passed away. And Roland handled all the details for the funeral. I had you and the boys to think about. Your uncle was a great help." Karin hears the defensiveness in her mother's voice. "I don't know how I would have coped without him."

There is something in her mother's voice that has Karin fingers tightening around her phone. "Mum..." She forces herself to continue. "Did you and Uncle Bernie have a thing going back then?" There is silence on the other end of the phone. "Mum?"

"It was a crazy time. Your father was away a lot: back and forwards to Perth, travelling to America, working on his new technology. You used to cry yourself to sleep when he was away."

"So Uncle Bernie stepped in."

"It wasn't like that—well, I suppose it was." Karin hears the doubt in her voice. Then her mother sighs, like she is relieved she has finally said it aloud—that the burden she has been carrying for so long is lifted. "Yes. I guess he did."

Karin's hand stills. She is not sure she can even take notes anymore. Uncle Bernie and her mother. An affair. She cradles Trouble like he can protect her from the hurt. Her own family, the people she is supposed to be able to trust most in the world, have been lying to her forever.

She needs to distance herself. Be professional. "How long did we stay in town after Dad died?"

"I don't know. While we packed up, I guess. What kind of question is that, anyway?"

She pictures her mother frowning into the phone, gathering her vague persona around her like it will protect her from anything Karin might say. This time, it won't.

"Did Uncle Bernie help us move? Or was it Aunt Julia? She was your friend, wasn't she?" Not that they had kept in touch, as far as Karin knows. She has never thought about her mother having friends. Or lovers. Her mother had disappeared inside herself after her father died, and it is only now that Karin wonders if it had been deliberate.

"I thought you were up there for Jess's wedding, not to dig up old hurts."

But Karin is not about to let her off the hook so easily. "Why didn't you stay in touch with Aunty Julia if she was your best friend?"

"I was upset. Your father died. I just wanted to forget. Why are you asking so many questions about an old photo anyway?"

And Karin knows she will not get anything more from her mother right now. "No reason. Just curious, I guess. Thanks for your help, Mum. Go back to your tea and cake. I've got to let Trouble out. He's scratching at the door."

Karin cuts off the call and cradles the dog to her side. So many lies. It is hard to know who to trust anymore. And there is the weekend at the Maskell's station to get through.

Damascus Rose, what have you done?

Chapter 17

"TELL me again why we're climbing a mountain at sparrow-fart in the middle of a heatwave?" Bec is leaning on her car in the small gravel parking area at the base of the track leading up the mountain. She looks at Karin, her gaze narrow.

Jess, too, is looking at Karin like she has forgotten to attach her brain to her fingers when she text them at five o'clock this morning. "If this is your idea of girl-bonding you had better have bought breakfast."

Bec turns to Jess. "And if you break into a run, I will have to kill you."

Jess is wearing indigo sports sweats, matching headband and joggers, her sleek black hair pulled back in a ponytail. She is rocking on the balls of her feet like she is limbering up for a race. Bec looks arty grunge in an oversized shirt and leggings, paint-splattered sandshoes that were once white, and there are charcoal smears on her fingers like Karin's phone call had dragged her away from her easel. Karin looks down at her own choice of attire and cringes. Branded hiking gear bought online from Paddy Palin. She is as out of place as any tourist who has flocked to the outback to take photos of themselves titled, "today I climbed a mountain" to post on Facebook.

Jess puts one leg forward and stretches her calf muscle before switching to the other leg. "Tell me again how you and Lukah got distracted yesterday instead of choosing a location for my wedding ceremony."

Bec pulls a muesli bar out of her pocket and rips the top open. "Methinks they may have gotten down and dirty at a certain pool with a deck and waterfall."

"Stop it you pair. I need to save my breath." Karin looks up at the mountain's ridge with its steep sloping sides and groans. "I don't remember this thing being so high."

"That's because the last time any of us were stupid enough to climb it was twenty years ago."

Karin glares at her dog who is circling them and barking, his leash tangling around Jess's ankles as she stretches. "At least one of us is enjoying ourselves." She unhooks his leash and shoos him ahead of her. With a glance upwards, she sighs and turns to trudge after him.

"Are you telling me this is your idea of a bridal party bonding activity?" Bec asks, swallowing the last of her muesli bar and wiping her hands on her shirt. "Or have you dragged us out here at ungodly o'clock so that you can show off your fancy new duds with the price-tag still attached."

Karin snatches at the back of her shorts with her free hand but there is nothing there. "Very funny. I dragged you out here because I've got something important to tell you."

"Have you ever heard of text messages?"

Karin doesn't know what to say. Her friends are right. But how can she tell them she doesn't want to look at the place where a woman fell to her death on her own.

She whistles to the dog. "Trouble, get back here." He ignores her as she knows he will, but it was worth a try.

"Got him well-trained, I see." Jess smirks as she pushes past and breaks into a jog.

"Sometimes," Karin mutters and glares at her friend's back who is already too far ahead to hear any snarky reply she can come up with.

The bride-to-be makes running up the mountain look like a stroll along the Swan River on a Sunday afternoon as she rock-hops and scrambles up the steep ascent at the start of the track, before settling into a rhythm as she follows the trail upwards. Trouble happily keeps her company, sometimes in front of her and sometimes behind, depending on his interest in whatever moves in the spinifex.

Bec's progress is steadier as if she is used to hiking but is happy to settle to her own rhythm and her own thoughts.

Karin is left to come up the rear, wondering why the hell she thought this was a good idea in the first place. Like everything else that has happened since she arrived in town, she has forgotten that living in the Pilbara breeds a certain kind of hardiness, and that in the city it is easy to become complacent.

Had Damascus Rose felt like that on the mountain? That life in the outback was too brutal and she decided to escape the only way she knew how?

Karin can only imagine the fallout from such an event. On her mother. On Julia Maskell. And all their husbands. She needs to tell her friends because the burden of knowing what happened to the woman in the photo is too much for her to carry alone. Her steps slow as if by dragging things out she can lessen the impact of what she is about to share. *A woman jumped off the mountain in front of our mothers and they never said a word.*

By the time Karin reaches the ridge where the trail evens out to a gentler rise, the others are waiting for her. They have their water bottles out and Bec is cupping her hands while Jess pours water into them for Trouble, who slurps with thankful joy then spoils it by drooling on her leg.

Jess wipes off the worst of the slobber with her hand and swings her pack around to her front. "Lucky I'm a planner." She unzips her and pulls out a pack of Wipes and Ziplock bag of trail mix.

"You call that sustenance? You clearly haven't had kids." Bec opens her pack and pulls out a container divided into four. There is watermelon, grapes, pistachio nuts and chocolate. "Who goes hiking without chocolate?"

Karin laughs. At least one thing hasn't changed. Jess the athlete. Bec the mother. And Karin determined to get the top regardless of what it takes. She looks up at how far they still have to climb and decides that makes her ambitious.

She chooses six squares of chocolate and a token grape. "This is a metaphor for my life," she says sadly.

"What, chocolate?"

"No. I think I've stuffed up my life."

Jess and Bec look at each other.

"Is this a midlife crisis?" Jess picks a slice of watermelon from the container. "Is it why you're drifting around the countryside in a hippy van instead of ladder-climbing in the big city?"

"I'm here for your wedding." Karin is affronted on behalf of her sleek charcoal Mercedes Vito Campervan that no hippy could afford. "And I'll have you know I'm travelling in style."

"We have an airport. Civilised guests fly in. They don't drive two thousand kilometres and then set up camp in a dustbowl paddock for weeks on end."

"It's called a Tourist Park and I'm on a working holiday," Karin mutters.

Bec and Jess exchange glances again.

"I thought you weren't going there," Bec says finally.

Karin shrugs. "What can I say? A story found me while I wasn't looking. Dad's story. It's just that the more I dig the more confused I get." She hesitates but these are her friends, and they deserve the truth. "It seems that everywhere I look the evidence is either missing or contradicts itself. My own family won't corroborate the facts about what happened the night he died. And my one real source sneaks around in the night with his headlights off like he's got something to hide. Either that or he's batshit crazy. What if Dad was right and I'm not up to it? That I can't get close enough to the real culprit because he's protected by an old boys' network that I'll never be privy to?"

Bec groans. "Not that old chestnut again."

"The chestnut that says you're not good enough." Jess at least had the sense to look commiserating. "Didn't you get over that when your investigative expose put all those white-collar criminals behind bars? I remember seeing pictures of you at the Walkleys weighed down by great big trophies."

"I had a team working with me. And a Corporate expenses account. Here, it's just me, the daughter of a man who worked here once. With zero access to anything important. Like evidence. I feel like the bad guys are watching me and laughing."

"What about if your Dad's death was an accident like everyone says," Bec points out. "And there is no story."

"You could end up being a hobo, drifting from town to town and raiding local garbage bins for day old bread and tomatoes with rotten spots," Jess suggests. "You could write stories about surviving in the wild and start your own reality YouTube channel."

"Stop it. I'm serious. I've spent years proving he was wrong. Fighting the bad guys. Taking them down. But I never did the one thing I should have done."

"And what's that?"

"Found out what really happened to my father that night and why everybody is being so evasive, even fifteen years after the fact."

"That's settled then," Bec says with a shrug, looking over Karin's shoulder. "Your fate is sealed. Karin Baxter, hobo on the road to nowhere, living sadly ever after in a fancy van with a dog who knows shit about staying out of trouble. Is that why you named him that?"

Karin follows Bec's gaze only to stare in horror as she watches Trouble balance on a narrow track winding up the side of the ridgeline. One false move and the dog is done for.

"No, don't call him," Bec warns. "Right now he has no idea of the shit he's in. If you call him and he actually listens to you and tries to turn around, he's either going to learn to fly real quick or he's done for.

Let him keep going. Look, he'll be past the narrow bit in a minute. There. You can open your eyes now."

Karin opens her eyes and lets out her breath. Trouble is twenty metres above them, sitting safely on a plateau and looking down at them like he is clever.

Jess frowns up at the dog before returning her attention to Karin, her gaze thoughtful. "I thought Lukah was your story. Or are you just using him for his body."

Karin is grateful for the change of topic. "I'm saying nothing in relation to his sexy-arsed body in case it incriminates me," she says lightly. "And I'm definitely not dallying with his affections. He knows the score. We had a conversation like civilized adults. We're enjoying a no-strings in-the-moment liaison."

"Tell us more," Bec says, munching on watermelon and washing it down with chocolate. "While we climb this hell-hole mountain. Spare no detail. We've got a long climb ahead and we're not mountain goats like your dog."

"I'll tell you while we're walking." Karin takes a swig of water and looks up. "I spoke to Mum last night."

"And?"

She turns around and holds up her phone. Bec and Jess gather around and look down.

"Damn, I was hoping I was going to see a picture of you and Lukah doing the good bits."

"Stop it," Jess scolds. "I think she's serious."

The two women look at Karin expectantly.

She swallows. "Recognise anyone in the photo?"

Jess shrugs. "Our parents. Doing whatever it was the parents did back in the day."

Karin realises that Jess lives in a different world where dressing to the nines and attending fancy functions is just another day for her.

When Karin had seen the photo, she was shocked to see her parents dressed like that. To Jess, it's nothing unusual.

"My father never wore a tuxedo in his life as far as I knew."

Bec laughs. "Or mine. But I can tell you one thing about those dresses. They don't come cheap. Even vintage they're thousands. Especially the maroon one in the middle." Bec snatches the phone out of Karin's hand. "Stunning," she murmurs. "Who's the woman."

"That's why we're here." Karin says. She continues walking, the others scrambling behind her. She comes to a halt at the Lion's Club compass. "Our mothers used to come up here," she says softly. "At least mine and Jess's did." She looks apologetically at Bec.

Bec shrugs. "My olds were cool even back then. Too cool to be seen in penguin suits and prissy party frocks."

The three women smile. Bec's parents are exactly as Bec says. Down to earth, which is where Bec gets her vibes from.

"You're lucky," Jess says softly. "We dress for dinner on a nightly basis. In clothes that need to be ironed."

"Poor little rich girl," Bec scoffs. "I bet you're not complaining now you have Grayson at your beck and call."

Jess grins. "I earned him. Try living with your parents when you're thirty-two years old. I can't wait to get married just so I can leave home."

"Shock horror. You know you'll have to do your own cooking and washing when the time comes."

Jess frowns and says nothing.

"Maybe when you married, your business will be able to afford some hired help," Karin says. "From what I hear J&J Constructions has a pretty good reputation."

"Did you hear what you just said? J&J. Jessalyn and Julia. My mother even follows me to work. It's like I'm a prisoner in my own life. And you think you've got it bad."

Karin has been so wrapped up in her problems she has forgotten that Jess, too, has problems. In the city her colleagues had joked about her one-track mind, her obsessive work ethic. Worse, she has involved her friends without thinking of how it will impact them.

Bec shoots Karin a scathing look and turns towards the crag. "Come on, Trouble. Let's go look at the view now that some nincompoop has dragged us all the way up here to see it."

Bec's right. Jess has enough to worry about with her adding to the pile with half-baked theories about events that happened years ago. It is time to explain her crazy behaviour, but she is more cautious now. They are no longer teenagers sharing everything about their lives. She straightens. She has worked on stories before. She knows how to be professional. But she is a little sad as she places a mental wall between her and her friends. It had been nice to come back and pretend everything was the same. Nothing is the same. And she makes a note to remind herself of the fact.

She turns to Jess. "It is pretty specky," she says, holding out her hand to her friend. "Shall we?"

She forces herself to focus on the golden light reflecting off the rocky outcrops. She had forgotten how spectacularly the Pilbara sun rose across the mountain ranges as it caressed the dips and valleys that stretched for miles across the landscape. Later, the sun will rise high in the sky and the heat will kick in for real, forcing people indoors as they seek blessed relief in their air-conditioned offices.

"Bring your phone over here," Bec calls from where she and Trouble are perched on a crag overlooking the town. "Take a photo to show Arno how outdoorsy we are."

"I don't suppose you'd consider bringing my dog away from the edge anytime soon?" She has seen too many sunrises lately, she tells herself. But there is another reason hovering in the shadow of her mind. The shadow forms a shape. The shape of a woman falling to her death. It is a long way down. Karin doesn't want to look. "Come away—"

Her protest comes too late. Jess is tugging at her hand. "Great idea, Bec. Come on, scaredy cat. Let's get one of the three of us."

Karin blocks the image of Damascus Rose as she smiles with her friends for the photo. Jess is right about one thing. It is a stunning view with flecks of light haloing clumps of spinifex that cling to the ridgeline and disappear over the rocky outcrops to the valleys below. She does not look down. She doesn't want to see.

"Hey, I can see your work." Bec points towards the curve of the railway line to the north of town. "Your Mum is already there." She elbows Jess's shoulder as Jess angles her phone to take their photo. "Which makes you late."

"Probably," Jess says with a grin. "One of the many benefits of my upcoming nuptials is she's signing the business over to me and retiring. I'll be free."

"Well, sort of... You'll have a new dragonslayer called a husband."

Karin sighs. "Can you pair stop blathering. I've got something serious to tell you." She feels her friends' gazes settle on her face and she forces her lips into a smile shape. "Sorry, too abrupt, huh?"

Jess snaps their photo and lowers her phone. "Yep. Got it in one."

Karin drops onto her arse beside Trouble and leans her head against him. And waits till her friends settle either side of her. "The woman in the picture, she fell from this spot."

Automatically, the three women look down. It is like Karin's words have conjured up the vision of a woman with sleek black hair that shined like raven's could grow wings and swoop down along the line of the mountain and fly off into the valley with one graceful dive.

Until they realise that women do not fly.

They fall.

They bleed.

And sometimes they do not survive.

"You can't be serious?" Bec is the first to recover and she is incredulous.

"That's what Mum told me." Karin draws up her legs and wraps her arms around her knees. "She said that she fell."

Jess is staring down into the valley, mesmerised. "Bernoulli's Principle," she says softly. "It would be a nice way to go, I think. Drifting down like a bird in a wind pocket."

Bec's response is dry. "If she was applying scientific principles, she forgot the bit about lift, you know, flapping her wings in order to soar."

"Maybe she didn't want to," Jess murmurs. "Maybe she was tired."

"Are we still talking about birds?" Bec glares at Karin over Jess's head.

See what you've done AGAIN.

I don't know what you're talking about.

She's stressed to the max about the wedding and you talking about dying is not helping.

Karin turns to Jess, blocking Bec's accusatory glare. "Mum said they came up here the night it happened. To watch the sunset while their husbands worked. They were drinking." She pauses. "And there may have been drugs involved."

Jess holds up a hand as if she can ward off Karin's words. "No," she says. "You can't be serious." She looks across the valley to the town where her mother is already at work, doing the only thing Jess can imagine her doing. She shakes her head as if to dislodge the image of her mother acting out of character and turns to glare at Karin. "Just no."

"Vermouth," Karin recants. "They were drinking vermouth out of a green bottle. Mum called it Green Vermouth like she knew what she was talking about."

"My mother—our mothers—and alcohol and drugs, all in the same sentence. No way."

Bec is watching Karin through narrowed eyes. "You're not joking, are you?"

Karin stares back silently. She should not have brought them up here. Should not have told them. Only she needed to. And now it is done.

"I'm sorry. I wish I was."

Trouble takes the moment to lean his head on her knee and remind her he is here. She scratches his ears and looks down. She keeps her tone neutral. "After she fell, they tidied up the mess and never spoke of it again." She remembers her mother's voice when she talked of the photo and hears again the anger in her voice, anger mixed with a sorrow so heartfelt Karin thought her mother was going to break. "I broke a rule I didn't know existed when I asked her about the photo."

Jess is silent so long Karin is not sure she is listening. Finally, she says, "Our parents really knew how to hide their sins, didn't they? All these years we've been idolizing them. Like they're some kind of saints."

"And that our childhoods were normal," Bec adds. "Well, I know mine was but I'm not sure about either of yours anymore."

Karin hesitates. "If they lied about that, what else have they lied about?"

"Wait," Bec says. "We only have your mother's word, and only because she's worried you'll find out anyway. What if she's still lying?"

"I agree," Jess says, her voice stronger. "If it really happened, if the woman did fall, then how come we never heard about it when we were kids? This is a small town, and rumours thrive in the place."

"Like the rumour that my father fell under a train, you mean? That kind of rumour?"

"If you like," Jess says. "Rumours have swirled for years about your father's death. But the first we knew about this woman is from you, today. No rumours. Nothing. Until you turn up with your version of a story you don't even know to be true. Is that how journalism works nowadays. Write the story, slot in facts you find convenient, no matter who gets hurt in the process?"

There are unshed tears mixed with anger in Jess's voice and Karin doesn't need Bec's glare to make her feel bad. Because Jess is right. She is the one telling the story. Dragging up the past. Upsetting her friends. Saying bad things about their parents.

Accusing.

She tries to speak but no words come out.

She looks helplessly at Bec who takes pity on her. "What's the woman's name? I can ask Dad and see if he remembers anything."

Karin sighs. "Damascus Rose."

It is Jess who looks at her this time, a frown marring her forehead. "Damascus, you say?"

"Does it ring a bell?" Karin is wary. Hopeful.

Jess frowns. "I normally pay zero attention to Dad's business dealings, but that name, I've heard it before. Show me the photo again."

Karen opens her phone and scrolls to the photo of their parents. She passes it to Jess.

Jess stares at the photo silently, then passes the phone back to Karin. "I could be wrong," she says, "but I think the man standing next to the woman is Senator Flint. I've heard Dad and him talking about one of their Companies, Damascus Holdings. And before you ask, I have no idea what the Company does."

The three women sit in silence; the dog still pressed against Karin's side. None of them speak because there is nothing to say that makes any sense.

"I came for a wedding," Karin says.

Bec smiles grimly. "That was the idea. But things seem to have gotten complicated since you arrived."

"The problem is," Jess says, "if you go all in on the story none of us might like what you find."

Karin nods. "Not to mention that the very people who have gone to so much effort to hide their secrets may well be on your guest list."

Jess drops her chin onto her chest. "Grayson thinks we should elope and I'm starting to wonder whether he's right."

"Might be the easiest way," Bec agrees. "I bags the three-piece orchestra and the honeymoon suite for me and Arno. Karin, you can babysit the kid and the dog, and me and Arno can have an all-expenses paid dirty weekend courtesy of the elopers. What? It'd be a shame to let all that decadence go to waste at this late stage. You won't get your money back, so we'd be doing your folks a favour."

"Or I could drop the story." Karin points out the obvious, hating to spoil Bec's fun but doing what she can to put a smile back on Jess's face. "And the wedding goes ahead as scheduled with nobody any the wiser about what we know." She is rewarded with a tremulous smile from Jess and an exaggerated moue from Bec.

"You had to spoil the dream, didn't you. Oh, well. I'll just have to rock my man's socks when we get off this damn mountain. If we hurry, I can meet him at the door naked when he gets off nightshift."

"Sounds like a plan." Jess pushes to her feet and extends her hands to her friends. "Shall we get to it?" She turns to Karin. "Or do you have more surprise news for us?"

"Well, there is one other thing I forgot to mention."

"Let me guess," Bec says. "Not only are me and Arno not getting a dirty weekend, but I'm not going to get my nookie this morning because you have another girl-bonding activity you can't wait for us to try."

"Mum has thirty million in a bank account in a shoebox in her bottom of her wardrobe."

Her statement is greeted with stunned silence. Then, without quite knowing how, the three of them are laughing, and it is only Bec's mothering instincts that herds them off the outcrop and onto firm ground before they're laughing so hard, Karin's worried Jess is going to cry again.

"Money," Jess says, pulling herself together with an effort. "The root of all evil."

"Says she who has more of the stuff than she knows what to do with, then adds insult to injury by marrying into more of it." Bec points her finger at the bride-to-be in mock outrage.

"I hope it's a Dolce & Gabbana shoebox." Jess says to Karin, ignoring the finger point with a lift of her chin.

"Designer name-dropping Rich bitch," Bec snarks.

"Op-shopping anti-snob," Jess returns, unperturbed.

"Break up the cat fight, girls. We've still got to get down the mountain and I, for one, need my energy for the climb."

Jess limbers up with an exaggerated stretch and breaks into a jog, calling over her shoulder. "See you at the bottom, losers."

Trouble, sensing the fun, lopes after her.

"So," Bec rustles around in her pack and brings out two chocolate bars and passing one to Karin, "What's on your agenda for the day now that you won't be wandering around town upsetting the locals by nosing around in their business?"

Karin grabs a bar before Bec can change her mind and unwraps it. "I thought I might hang out at the Tourist Park and nose around in their business from the safety of the internet. That way they won't know I'm nosing and therefore they won't be offended." She shoves half the bar into her mouth, swings her pack onto her back, and starts after Jess and her dog.

"Ya reckon?" Bec calls after her as she zips her pack and slings it over her shoulder. "I give it a day. Tops. And you'll be the only one people are talking about. That Baxter brat is back meddling in business that doesn't concern her, while I get to fly under the radar for a change. Go for it, girl. I'm happy for it to be your turn. But be warned. They can be a vicious bunch. They'll will take you down and you won't see it coming, especially if you continue cavorting with the most eligible bachelor in town."

"By cavorting, you mean I get to play with his hunk of a bod while the local girls drool with envy?"

"That, too. I'm even a tad jealous of that part. But heads up, with your not-so-subtle sleuthing on top of waltzing out of Jess's hens' night with the town's most eligible bachelor, there can't be many people in town that you haven't offended."

"All I've done so far is turn up. Imagine what I can do if I try."

Bec groans and pushes past her. "The poor fucking town doesn't know what's about to hit it. Just remember, we're the bridesmaids and we're not supposed to outshine the bride. Save your fucking detective work until after the wedding, okay?"

"Okay." Karin tries for contrite but instead manages to choke on her chocolate.

If she's looking for sympathy she is out of luck. Bec has sailed past her and is sure-footedly pulling ahead. While Karin is left to wonder what has happened to the memory muscle of her childhood when she had been as sure-footed as a goat. It looked like her sure-footed has deserted her, like her friends and her dog have.

She finds herself left to her own thoughts as she half climbs and half slides back down the way she has come. Leaving her to ponder the link between mountains and goats and who the fool was who thought the two should be used in the same sentence.

Chapter 18

THE train moves to a beat, a rhythm, and the landscape accepts the sinuous dance of the metal giant rhumbaing up the long haul from Para and curving across the plains of the 7 Mile to Dampier where wagons of ore are crane-loaded into the jaws of open-mouthed ships at the rate of a million tonnes a day.

The noise spins around in your head, the friction of steel against steel at fifty degrees accentuating the high-pitched momentum of a train passing close to you in the dark.

Then it is on top of you, every wagon a demonic pitch to your brain as you lay hapless. The train splays your guts at a speed that cuts much deeper than its 75 km limit portends.

The wagons, too, are louder than you expect, like they are anchored more squarely on the rails after the bump, the noise of the hit reverberating in time with your last breath.

And then the train is gone, the pitch more even now as the engines settle into the task of delivering their dumpers to the sea.

Karin's hands are stiff is she sets up her laptop on the van's small table. Trouble is fed and watered, and asleep at her feet. They have climbed the mountain. Seen where a woman jumped to her death.

It is time to investigate her father's death. To write his story. And in doing so, she will expose another story, starting fifteen years before. To right a wrong. To give dignity to a woman whose story, for whatever reason, has not been told.

Her instinct tells her it will be big.

And Bec is right. She is being annoying with her questions.

Which tells her she is on the right track. People will try to stop her. Important people. But she has been there before, and the truth has prevailed. Her by-line is respected. And people will listen. She is just not sure who the bad guys are. Or who is most annoyed. Exposing bad guys to public scrutiny is a dangerous occupation.

Old Nev is not far wrong with his prophesy. She needs to be careful because he is not crazy. He is cunning. He wanted her to speak to her mother about the photograph, to find out about the death of Damascus Rose. To make the link between her father's death and the death of a woman fifteen years prior.

There are no coincidences in this story.

Only her own uncertainty, planted by her father all those years ago. Is she good enough? Only now, she knows this is not the right question. The real question is does she want to know?

She opens a new document and begins to type:

Are the wagons empty or full when they run over her father? At what point does the safety switch kick in and say there was something – someone – on the line? If he is alive, he will have seen – long before he felt – the sheer horror of what is about to happen to him. Is it enough for the men that did this to him? Or do they want more? Maybe they come back. And observe the fruits of their labour. Satisfaction at a job well done.

Preliminary search:

A man is dead, run over by his own train. The report is scant in its detail. There was something on the track. Nobody expected it to be a body. A magnet flicks and the train begins to slow but is it too late for the man who is splayed over the track – passed out maybe – from a punch to the head. King hit, they reckon. Some cowardly bastard hit him from behind and left him to bleed out on the track. Divine retribution, the blokes say over their beers. But they must have felt something for their old mate. A fuck of a way to die maybe or Jesus Christ, hope he was dead before the train hit.

A Tribute to a Legend says none of these things. She brings up the article in her notes. It calls him a hero and quotes accolades from his mates as social proof.

She works methodically, making notes, cross-referencing. Fact checking, she searches for the coronial file on the death of James Robert Baxter, but the file is sealed. By whom? Senior Next-of-Kin is the only person with the power to seal a file. Has her mother done this? Or has someone else made sure there be no access to the file containing police reports, witness statements, experts' reports, and the coroner's findings. She downloads an Access Application and makes a note to ask her mother.

She keeps digging. She types Train-Death-Hammersley-2009 into Trove. The West Australian newspaper brings up several hits. She copies and saves several links pertaining to the proposed Pilbara Auto-haul. But a dead man? Nothing.

She tries her father's name.

Obituary: *loving husband, father, brother* – there is no Latin epitaph in the newspaper.

There is a brief article from *Mining Monthly*:

The loss of one of mining's finest – killed in a train accident in the Pilbara. No suspicious circumstances. Condolences to the family.

The Mining Institute of Western Australia released an official comment. "Ore news from the Pilbara: accidental death of one of

Western Australia's own," followed by promises of changes to workplace health and safety.

Had James Baxter been working overtime?

The union stance is the mining company is cutting costs to the detriment of worker safety. Uncle Bernie is the mine's union representative. She has never heard him talk about the circumstances of her father's death. Or of the culpability of the mine. She adds the question to her notes.

After the accident, there is talk of a Parliamentary Inquiry into rail safety in the mines. Railways Commissioner for Mines, Gerald Summers, says, "All avenues will be explored to prevent future deaths," and that, "Mine safety is top priority."

There is no follow-up.

She scans through several months of the West Australian but there is nothing. Like the death has been forgotten.

Or buried.

Then she sees it; *Funding Approved for a Feasibility Study into the Auto-haul.* Her father's technology triumphs his death in the newspapers, with promises of "*the biggest single automated rail system in the world.*"

Share prices rise but not so much they cause a trading halt. Just enough to intimate a prosperous future for investors. The State Government takes quiet credit for the initiative. Senator Brandon Flint declares his interest as a member of the board of Starr Holdings, a major investor in the technology.

Brandon Flint, the man her mother identified as the husband of Damascus Rose, is a member of the Australian Senate, one of twelve Western Australian representing the State's interests. Openly declaring pecuniary interest in one of the biggest transport developments in West Australia's recent history. There is no mention of ethical concerns or conflict of interest. Karin makes a note, saves the article and moves on.

With a few clicks of her keyboard, she maps out the available information on Senator's private life. Private boarding school educated. Engineering Degree (Hon), from the University of Western Australia. Married to Lorena, a Law Professor at the same university, who continues to pursue her career in political law.

There is no mention of a first wife dying in 1993 from a cliff-fall in the Pilbara.

It takes another hour of solid research to unravel the Senator's political career. His donors. The Bills he is instrumental in having passed in the Senate. Esteemed. Accolades to a man who has achieved much and worked tirelessly for the good of the State of Western Australia.

Retired, 2020, to pursue private interests.

Currently serving on the boards of various public and private entities.

There is a portrait of the Senator on the walls of Parliament – served Queen and Country from 1995 to 2020.

Twenty-five years and a gold watch for his efforts.

And a spot on the Bulletin's Top 200 Rich List for twenty of those years. No wonder he is pissed that she is back in the town where it all began, asking questions he does not want answered anytime soon.

Her phone vibrates and she picks it up. "Hey."

"Hey yourself." Lukah's voice has her sitting back and stretching her cramped muscles. "Thought you might be in town, and I could shout you a coffee."

"Still at the Park, sorry."

"Working?"

"Yeah. Do you know how I get my hands on the coronial file on my father's death without filling out an Access Application?"

"Why, Ms Baxter. You wouldn't be asking me to do anything illegal, would you?"

Karin stares out the van window, frowning. "It was worth a try. I don't seem to be getting far with my online access efforts. Mostly dead-ends, and Parliamentary Inquiries going nowhere."

"You think someone's burying the paper trail?"

"I'm starting to wonder if there is a paper trail. I can't even access the Mine's report on the incident. It's like the accident never happened."

"They would have kept it under wraps. A death on a mine-site is never a good look."

"Even from the local police?"

"Darlin', I'm compromised. They know I'm yours. I doubt they'd let me near any records, but I should be able to bring up what our investigating officers found when they were called to the incident."

"It's a start," she says, "but I'm guessing whoever did this would have covered their tracks by now."

"Or they got careless after all this time."

"Maybe," she says.

"Which is why I'm calling. I think we should put a protective detail on you."

"For being in town for my girlfriend's wedding?"

"Well, when you say it like that – I was thinking of a more personal detail. Like you come and stay at mine till the wedding."

She laughs. "You want me to move in with you so you can protect me."

"I can think of worse reasons."

"Okay."

"Okay what?"

"Okay, I'll think about it."

"Just think about it?"

"The idea of a flushing toilet and a tap with running water has certain appeal."

"Sheesh, and not my body?"

"Like I said, I'll think about it." She is smiling as she ends the call. "What do you reckon, Trouble. Are we tempted by the man's offer or are we doing just fine on our own?"

The dog's tail twitches as he rolls over and falls back to chasing rabbits in his sleep. So much for consensus. Looks like this is one decision she will be making on her own. She turns back to her laptop and tries not to think about what compromising the local policeman would involve.

Chapter 19

"HOLD on to your hats, ladies. The wind is on our side and this baby's ready to fly." Jess sits in the cockpit of the chopper in front of instruments and gauges while Bec sits beside her calmly adjusting her seatbelt.

Karin is in the back trying not to think about becoming airborne in case she embarrasses herself by throwing up before they leave the ground. Did these things have handles she can cling to? Anything? She can't remember. She closes her eyes and counts to fifty. Opens them a peep and closes them again. She needs another fifty to steady her breathing. Jess is a great pilot. The best. Intellectually, Karin knows that counts for something. Her stomach, on the other hand, has lost contact with her brain and is beginning to heave.

The weekend has come around too quickly. She is not ready to face the Maskells knowing what she knows, which is both too much and nothing at all in relation to her father's death. Despite scouring the internet, calling in favours and ringing total strangers who happened to work with her father once upon a time, she has learning little about why he was driving a train that night when his role on the roster was listed as Supervising Engineer. Least of all how he ended up dead under its wheels. Meeting the Maskells, looking Roland Maskell in the eye, and making small talk after all these years will cost her every bit of her hard-earned professional veneer.

And some.

And that's after she tosses her cookies.

She is not ready, will never be ready, but here she is, bleary eyed, with a smile plastered on her face, ready to fly. *I am a bridesmaid. Jess is my friend. I am a bridesmaid. I can do this.* "Err... I feel sick."

"We haven't taken off yet, idiot." Bec swings around from the front seat and passes her a Mintie. "Here, suck on this and stop being a baby."

After completing their pre-takeoff checklist, Jess passes Bec a headset. "Sit back and enjoy the scenery," she says over her shoulder to Karin. "We'll be at Windelema in twenty minutes."

"Beats catching a bus." Bec fiddles with her seatbelt, adjusts her headset, and turns to check on Karin. "You okay back there? Need Mama's help?"

Karin sighs. Giving Bec the front seat was a mistake but one she can't take back. And Bec is crowing like the proverbial cockerel. "Just remember research shows it's you that hit the ground first when we crash land."

"Testy this morning, aren't we," Bec replies. "Didn't get your coffee delivered by a certain copper, hey?"

Damn. If Bec knows Lukah has been spoiling her with early morning deliveries of coffee and Danishes, then the whole town knows. "I gave him the morning off so I could listen to your dulcet tones ragging me out."

"Lucky for you I did a pickup on the way to the hangar. Look in the Esky beside you. Coffee to go, and I heard Apricot Danish is the flavour of the month."

Bec grins as she turns back to the front and shares a high-five with Jess. But Karin is past caring about being the butt of their joke. Steaming hot coffee is the only thing that will restore her humour. She undoes the lid of the Esky and breathes in the aroma of caffeine.

The coffee, along with a Danish, is enough to get her through takeoff. She relaxes into her seat as best she can and stares out the window.

Jess steers a course along the contours of the Hammersley Range. They are headed towards the Millstream where her family's station stands testament to her forebears who, with tenacity and struggle, forged a cattle empire that has made Windelema one of the pre-eminent stations in the Pilbara.

It isn't the first time Karin and Bec have joined Jess for a visit. During their school holidays, Jess's father would often drop them out at the station in the chopper, return to his job at the mine, and do the same round trip at the end of the holidays. Jess's mother would play hostess to the girls as they played tennis, rode horses or, weather permitting, hung out down at the river reading their books and discussing their future dreams. The last mostly centred around boys. They never thought about what it was like for Jess's mother when there was nobody around with nothing for her to do except tend her gardens and play the grand piano Jess's great grandfather had brought to Windelema on the back of a wagon a century ago.

They had been young and carefree.

And privileged, she realises now.

Everything had changed, at least for Karin, after her father died and she had moved to the city. Long lazy days with her friends had given way to a frenetic determination to succeed at her chosen career, starting with her university studies, and followed by her immersion in the world of economics and business, where she learned fast that white collar crime was a thing and that for the most part, it was sanctioned by those who profited most, even if some business activities erred on the wrong side of legal.

The pub around the corner from the Australian Securities Exchange in Georges Terrace became her local hangout and the brash young dealers on the stock market floor with more money than sense, her friends.

Most of those young men now held positions of power, influence, or both, in the intimate world of finance in Australia's most isolated state, Western Australia.

It made her progress to the top of the pile at the Economist relatively painless. She took her colleagues' ribbing that she had slept her way there with equanimity.

Jess earned her pilot's license young. Everyone out this way did. After university, she set up her own business, J&J Engineering. When lucrative mining contracts came her way due to her family connections, nobody pointed the finger. It was the way things worked in the outback.

And now Jess is about to make a marriage that merged two of the district's biggest landholdings, in what is considered a closed circle of closely guarded wealth and privilege. Their upcoming nuptials are touted as one the best business deals around.

Karin has covered too many mergers not to be a little bit cynical. But Jess seems genuinely happy with Grayson.

Is she jealous of her friend? Not a bit. She likes her life in the city. She likes the rhythm of her days. But she is burnt out and she needs a break. And Jess's wedding is the perfect excuse. *You can fool some of the people some of the time.* She hates the voice that makes her doubt. She has earnt her reputation by asking the hard questions. But it is the first time the first question is addressed to herself. *Do you want to know?* Only then, can she look her best friend's father in the eye. *Mr Maskell, there are things that don't add up the night my father died. And all lines of questioning lead to you. Mind if I ask you why the supervising engineer was driving the train that night? Would you mind showing me the findings from the inquiry into his death?* She glances at the back of Jess's head and finally accepts she has crossed the line from personal to professional interest. *Look into my eyes, Mr Maskell, and show me your soul.*

Karin rests her head on the window and looks down at the passing landscape. Just because she has come to a decision, it doesn't make the execution any easier. She still needs to ask the questions her research demands of the man who covered up the details of what happened that night. And she is no longer a child where the grown-ups set the rules. Roland Maskell cannot brush her aside with platitudes about not worrying her pretty head. Just as she can no longer hide behind the lie that she does not want to know.

She watches as the station boundary fence that runs along the ridgeline of the Millstream National Park come into view. She is about to find out. She straightens as Jess brings the chopper down neatly onto the landing strip. A white Land Rover with a single occupant is waiting for them.

As they alight the chopper and move away from the rotor blades, Jess throws herself into her fiancé's arms.

Karin looks away.

Bec chuckles. "Come on, let's get this party started."

Bec has made no secret that she has been waiting for this weekend to do nothing but be waited on and hang out by the pool.

They step up onto the wide sweeping verandah as the front door opens. "Welcome," Jess's mother greets them with a smile. "You made good time."

"Jess wanted to beat the heat," Bec says, stepping forward to kiss Julia Maskell's cheeks, French style.

Karin hangs back, although she is not sure why. The older woman is dressed immaculately in white linen, her hair pulled into a bun and secured with a tortoiseshell clip. Offering Karin a cursory smile, she beckons them to enter and leads the way along an airconditioned hallway the main living area of the homestead. Karin looks around at the grand piano, the polished timber floorboards covered in an antique oriental rug, the family portraits of successive generations in gold frames on the walls, and the sweeping staircase leading to the second floor with its curved balustrades the girls had taken turns in sliding down when nobody was watching.

"Susie will show you to your rooms, girls. When you have freshened up, come down for a light snack." As she finishes speaking Jess bursts in the room and wraps her mother in a hug.

"Darling." Jess's mother offers her cheek, frowning slightly. "Such a display in front of our guests."

Jess winks over her mother's head at her friends. "It's okay, Mumsie. The girls are used to my crass ways. I'm looking forward to being home for a few days."

Karin sees the rings around her friend's eyes. "Julia was just sending us off to our rooms to freshen up."

Bec is already halfway up the stairs, running a hand along the polished balustrade. "I don't know why you bother working. With all this you could live the life and never lift a finger again."

Jess looks at Karin and they smile. They have heard Bec say this many times. Jess links her arms with Karin's, and they march Dorothy style up the stairs after her.

"Please don't let her slide down the balustrade while Mumsie's watching."

"She won't," Karin replies solemnly.

"She would," Bec interrupts their dialogue. "Except she wants to swim more. Pool or river, ladies?"

"Pool," Jess and Karin say in unison.

"We can have lunch out there if you like," Jess adds, looking back at her mother for confirmation.

Julia nods. "You girls enjoy yourselves. I'll sort lunch and have it brought out a bit later."

Jess turns back to her friends. "Other than the shindig tonight, we should be able to squeeze in some relaxing during the weekend."

Karin hears the weariness in her voice. "Is everything okay?"

"Mother likes all the fuss," Jess returns. "Me? I wish we could elope."

"And spoil a whole weekend where we don't have to lift a finger? Sorry, not happening." Bec skips up the final stairs like she is a teenager again. "Besides, if you elope, then you don't get to spend a whole weekend of quality time with us."

Karin and Jess catch up with Bec and the trio stand in front of an ornate mirror grinning like the teenagers they once were.

"You're right." Jess squares her shoulders, lifts her chin and stares solemnly into the mirror. "Elopement is off the bingo card. Got it."

"Excellent. Now to more important things." Bec steps forward, lifts the corner of her T-shirt and wipes an imaginary spec of dirt off the mirror, before falling back in line. "Mirror, mirror, on the wall," she says in her best elocution voice. "Who is the richest one of us all?"

"That'd be me." Jess steps forward, pokes her tongue out at the mirror, and steps back.

"And the fairest one of all?" Bec fluffs her hair and bows. "Me of course."

"Why do I always have to be the smartest one of all?" Karin makes round shapes with her fingers and places them at her eyes. "I want a turn at being the fairest one."

"She dies, remember?"

"Oh, yeah. In that case, maybe not."

"Enough chatter. Last one down at the pool is a rotten egg." Bec breaks rank, her gaze running along the hallway. "I'm guessing we still get our old rooms?"

Jess gestures towards a line of doors that lead to separate suites, all with French windows opening onto private balconies. "Of course. Nothing but the best for my fellow princesses. Except you, Bec. There's a pea under your mattress."

They are laughing as they go their separate ways to their rooms to change. Karin opens the door to the room she had a teenager and looks around room with its bay windows shut tight against the rising heat and its exotic flowers flown in from God knows where. Her case has been unpacked, and her things are put away in the same mahogany chest of drawers she used as a kid. On top of the drawers there is a towel for the pool and her swimsuit resting beside it.

It would be easy to get used to the luxury. But she can see how Jess might see things differently. Coming home entailed all the pressures of living up to perfection and Jess has done it all her life.

Karin almost feels sorry for her friend.

Almost.

She changes on her swimsuit, grabs the tow and heads to the pool.

Chapter 20

Lukah and Arno arrive in a four-wheel-drive mid-afternoon, with Toby in the back seat and Trouble hanging out the window.

"Two-hour drive," Lukah says to explain their lateness. "And we may have gotten off to a late start due to a certain buck's night."

Arno grins at Karin as Trouble jumps out the window into her arms and licks her face. Toby is already out of the car and racing towards the pool where Bec holds out her arms to him, then dunks him at the last minute.

It is their old gang back together.

With extras.

For the first time Karin can see Jess's future laid out in minutiae, trapping her in a life from which there is no escape like her mother before her. Karin can't help wondering how she would feel if this was her future.

As the afternoon heats up everybody disappears to various parts of the house to rest before dinner.

Karin knocks softly on Jess's door and enters.

Jess is standing at the French windows, looking out. "It never changes. This view. This place. I don't know how Mother stands it."

Karin flops on the bed and sinks back into cushions. "Oh, I don't know. This could be your lot one day."

"The weight of history is mine to bear, Daddy says."

"Is everything okay, Jess. You do want this, don't you?" She is half joking. "Who wouldn't?"

Jess turns around Karin sees the doubt. "I am lucky, aren't I? I've got it all."

"But?"

"The other night at Bec's," she says. "It was all so easy. Everyone clowning around, drinking beers, telling ribald jokes. Out here, look at us. We swim, rinse off, and eat fancy sandwiches with the crusts cut off. We retire during the heat of the afternoon, then change into our eveningwear as ordered, and dine under fucking chandeliers like we're someone important. It's all so fucking civilised."

Karin chuckles. "Methinks the bride has pre-wedding jitters. Don't worry. We're here to see you through. Bec's already breaking the rules. She's still in the pool with Arno and Toby. And Trouble's running around the edge, barking his head off. New traditions can be made. Things don't have to stay the same forever."

"In your world maybe." Jess doesn't move away from the window.

Karin swings her legs off the side of the bed and moves to take her friend's arm. "Sit with me."

She leads Jess to a pair of teal wingback chairs. Jess curls up in one chair and Karin stretches out on the other, lifting her feet onto a matching studded ottoman. She lets the silence sit between them, trusting Jess will talk when she is ready.

The room hasn't changed since the days when the three of them used to push the furniture aside and play Knuckles in the centre of the floral Persian rug. Large timber bookshelves line one wall and Karin recognises the Billabong, Nancy Drew and Trixie Beldon series had pored over as kids, with Jess's four-poster bed taking up one corner of the room. The fireplace is at the far end of the room with its marble mantle lined with family photographs in gold frames. It is stacked with wood and artfully arranged pinecones, as if the room would turn from mausoleum to cosy with the strike of a match.

For the first time since they arrived, Karin has an inkling of the responsibility Jess feels.

"It's like we're going through the motions." Jess looks at Karin as if she can see the dawning understanding in her friend's eyes and is wondering what took her so long. "Grayson is going along with his family's orders, the same as me with mine."

"Do you love each other?"

"I thought I loved him. I do love him. I'm just not sure I want to give up myself if you know what I mean."

"Isn't this a conversation you guys should have had before—"

"Before? You mean before we sign on the dotted line? I honestly thought I could do it. But now that it's real I'm suddenly not sure I can. Ridiculous, hey?"

Karin feels helpless against the weight of Jess's concern. "Your mother—"

"I don't want to end up like her."

They sit in silence and stare out the window at the miles of nothing. The afternoon heat creates a haze that shimmers across the red earth held together by spinifex and mulga scrub.

"I've never understood what would make anyone live out here in the first place," Jess muses. "And they're about to retire here. Mother's not happy about it but Daddy's away most of the time. They haven't had a chance to talk it out. At least when I was little, they liked each other—I think—but there is no saying that now."

"Remember the last time we visited and Bec did the whole loosening the sugar lid thing?

Jess smiles as Karin intends. "I can still remember the roasting I got. Daddy gave me this big lecture about responsibilities, and that it wasn't acceptable behaviour from a young lady in my position. Like I was the culprit, not Bec." She straightens and rubs her hands along her thighs, before admitting, "I don't think I can live up his expectations anymore. I'm not even sure I want to..." Her voice drifts off and she returns her gaze to the window.

The words hang between them like a confession and Karin is not sure how to reply. This is Bec's domain. Compassionate, practical, and calm-in-a-crisis Bec, who is swimming with Arno and Toby, unaware of that the bride is about to blow the marriage deal of a century, all for the want of the calming words from her other bridesmaid who, it seems, has the emotional maturity of a nit. "I think I should go get Bec—"

Jess's gaze swings back to Karin. "Sometimes I want to be like her, you know. With nothing more to worry about than who to invite for a barbecue and piss up."

"I'm not sure Bec would agree with your summation of her life. Besides, you'd get bored in five minutes. The Jess Maskell I know and love thrives on challenges."

"And that's the problem. Grayson wants us to take an extended trip to America after the wedding. Like I can just drop everything and go with him. My business, the place I've built from scratch, apparently doesn't mean anything in the scheme of things."

"When did he say this?"

"Him and Daddy have been working on a deal over there, and it's Grayson job to finalise it. As his wife, I'm supposed to be at his side. I never wanted to be somebody's accessory."

"Grayson is a good man," Karin returns quietly. "Have you told him how you feel?"

"Of course. But we both know this whole marriage thing isn't about us. It's about the alliance of two family dynasties." Bec rests her head on the wing of her chair and looks at Karin. "Remember how we used to dream about marrying the perfect handsome hero and how we would recognise him because he would sweep us off our feet and leave us with no doubt that he was the one. Well, guess what? That's not how it works. We sign contracts and make deals. How do we live happily ever after with all that crap hanging over us?"

"They same way your parents did, maybe? Compromise and common goals?"

"I don't remember the word compromise being part of our dreams. We were going to take on the world and win."

"But we're older how, and wiser. Your parents' marriage survived in the real world, not some teenage fantasy utopia."

"There was a time when they were happy. Back in the beginning. But not anymore. It makes me wonder whether following in the family tradition is the holy grail of happiness I've always been told it would be."

"You can still take on the world." But Karin is less sure now.

"I think you're questioning the fairytale, too. You've opted out of the fantasy altogether, drifting around, doing nothing. Not exactly the taking-on-the-world kind of stuff we dreamed about when we were kids."

"That's mine and Trouble's lives you're talking about." Karin tries desperately to lighten the mood, but she is afraid her friend is right. *Bec, where are you?* This is a full-on crisis needing all bridesmaids on deck.

"Tell me that's not what you're doing," Jess continues, leaning forward and drilling Karin with her gaze. "You turn up here in your hippy van with a dog for fuck's sake. God knows how that happened."

"I felt sorry for him, so I liberated him from the local shelter. And I've taken leave, not dropped out." She wonders if crossing her toes is the same as crossing her fingers behind her back. "Besides, my life's different to yours, Jess. My father's the dead one, remember? You still have your family and you're marrying into another one."

Silence sits uncomfortably between them, and Karin has no idea how to break it.

"I'm hoping this is just pre-wedding jitters," she says finally.

"Me, too." Jess sighs. "Me, too."

Chapter 21

I T IS a family dinner unlike any Karin has experienced.

Julia Maskell has outdone herself. The walnut table is extended to fill the dining room. It is covered in a white French linen tablecloth. There are three centrepieces of ice-carved rose blooms surrounded by buds of diamantes set in gold, with gold stems supporting the ice roses.

The sculptures are intricate in their design. And impressive. A demask table runner in charcoal grey has rose petals in various shades of burnt orange and sunset yellows scattered along its length. A single gold candelabra reflects the light of the ice roses, giving the whole an elegance that Karin stares at in open-mouthed admiration. She could be at the fanciest restaurant in Perth and it would be left wanting against Julia Maskell's touch.

Roland Maskell is at the head of the table with his wife at the other end. There is a slight shuffling of the personalized place cards as Bec sits herself, Arno and Toby together. Lukah picks up his and Karin's place cards from opposite sides of the table and places them next to each other before holding out a chair for her with a half-bow from his waist. Jess hesitates and does the same with hers and Grayson's place cards. She is smiling softly as if the small rebellion is daring, except Karin sees the covered glance she shoots towards her mother.

Julia's gaze gives nothing away, but her back is straight as she takes her place at the end of the table.

Bec is guileless as she leans over Toby to straighten his napkin, taking the opportunity to whisper to him as he is pulls faces at his polished silverware. Karin suppresses a smile as he pokes out his tongue, then huffs on the knife to watch it fog. Bec straightens, not sure she likes being outdone by her son, and Karin wonders if she is going to join him and make it a competition.

Karin crosses her fingers that Bec doesn't give into temptation, and Arno obviously thinks the same because he takes Bec's hand in his and places it on his thigh.

He winks at Karin and the crisis is averted.

For now.

"Good to see you girls again," Roland says jovially, unaware of the byplay between his guests and wife. He smiles at his daughter's friends, but there is a wariness in his eyes as his gaze rests on Karin's and moves on, then swings back to her.

It takes all her effort not to squirm under his gaze.

"How long are you in the Pilbara?" His tone is light.

Karin offers a smile. "Just here for the wedding," she says. "Then moving on."

"Jess says you've resigned your job." A polite question accompanied by curious gaze.

Karin meets his gaze with an openness that tries for disarming but is more like a grimace. "All work and no play were starting to take its toll on my mental health," she replies. "I thought a road trip for Jess's wedding was the perfect opportunity to reset while I decide on new directions."

"There is always a job for you here."

Keep your friends close and your enemies closer. The expression hits her so hard she drops her gaze, unable to formulate a reply.

Jess comes to her rescue. "No work talk, remember," she says lightly. "You promised."

Her father shrugs, leans back in his chair and lifts his glass of red to his lips. "Sorry darling. Thought I was helping."

Jess's mother, recovered from Bec's prank, takes up the mantel from her husband. "Chef's done a wonderful job tonight," she says brightly, but there is a brittle edge in her voice. "Peter is here to serve. No need to help yourselves." She looks pointedly at Bec who is about to do just that.

As she speaks a man in a tuxedo who has been standing by the sideboard steps forward and lifts the lids off the various tureens. Another waiter is busy offering wines, red or white, a serviette over his forearm, the labels of the wines showing to each guest in turn.

A woman enters from the kitchen and places a crystal glass of juice in front of Toby. Bec promptly reaches into her tote and pulls out a plastic mug, tipping the juice into it and passing it to her son. She hands the crystal glass back to the woman.

Bec is at her irrepressible best. "Remember the good old days," she says. "We used to get up to all sorts of mischief out by the pool during these formal dinners. I've gotta admit I quite like sitting at the grown-up table." She drains her wine glass and holds it out the waiter. "Feel free to invite us to all your functions when you're the lady of the house, Jess."

Julia smiles, her expression unreadable. "I'm looking forward to the day." She turns to her daughter and her gaze softens. "Grandchildren will bring the place alive again."

Jess looks sideways at Grayson. "No pressure," she mutters.

Karin lifts a forkful of salmon pate to her mouth to stop herself laughing. Both friends were in rebellious moods, and if they aren't careful, they will all get sent to their rooms in disgrace.

She turns to her hostess. "Have you been to the city lately, Mrs Maskell? The new season's fashions were starting to hit the shops when I left."

Jess's mother took her cue. "I guess there's plenty of time for travel now that Jess is stepping up."

Jess's knuckles are white around her fork. "Nothing has been decided," she replies quietly. "Grayson and I still have some things to iron out, including the fact that I have a business to run."

"Don't be silly child," her father admonishes. "You can keep your business, just put someone in to manage it. Grayson will need you at his side when he travels."

"Hey, I'm here," Grayson says mildly. "I say we focus on the wedding and our honeymoon trip to America before we worry about other things." He raises Jess's hand to his lips. "There'll be time to worry about the rest later. Besides, I'm rather proud of having such a talented wife and life partner. I'm not sure I want her to give up her dreams for mine. But whatever we decide, you'll be the first to know, Sir."

Karin admires his effort at smoothing his fiancées ruffled feathers while at the same time appearing to appease his future father-in-law. She wonders how long he can keep walking the tight rope between love and duty.

One look at Jess's face and she realises she is about to find out. Pre-wedding jitters were about to erupt into a full-throttled thunderstorm. And Poor Grayson has no idea that his usually amiable fiancée is about to lose it.

She feels Bec's gaze on her.

Do something.

What?

I don't know. Anything. Bleed.

"I've heard there's a new merger between Fortesque and Macedena Holdings," Karin says desperately, trying to remember the gossip on the pub circuit. "Something to do with renewables and being at the forefront of the technology. It's causing quite a stir in financial circles."

Roland Maskell turns his attention to Karin. "Is that so? You must hear a lot of things in your line of work."

Thanks, Bec. Now he has me in his sights.

But in that moment, she recognises something else in his gaze. Curiosity? Vulnerability? Dislike? She sits back in her chair at the shock of it. All this time—all these years—she has believed her father when he said she would never be privy to the inner workings of the wealthy.

The truth hits her so hard she has to remember to breathe. She has been blinded by her own insecurities. She is not playing their game on their terms.

They need her.

It is her connections, and her ability to sift through the financial dealings of a business, and to come up with evidence that has been concealed. Or buried so deep it is impossible to recognise.

The moment she looks him in the eye, she knows.

And so does he.

As the man men chat take up the conversation Karin kicks Bec under the table. When Bec looks up she nods towards Jess.

Oh, okay, on it.

Karin waits while Bec engages Julia in a conversation about the catering for the wedding, and stares at Jess until she looks up from her plate.

You hanging in there?

Sure.

Jess drops her gaze to her dinner and turns her salmon over on her plate.

Karin places her knife and fork in the middle of her plate. "Hey, Jess, remember how when we were kids we'd go hang out in the library after dinner while the grown-ups talked business? Want to come rehash old memories and leave the guys to their guy talk?"

Jess stands without a word, as does Bec.

Julia is about to intervene, but she looks at Jess's face and nods. "Good idea. You girls go ahead. I'll have coffee is brought in." If she is disappointed the meal has ended so abruptly, she does not show it. "I might join you later. If that's okay?"

Jess is halfway out the door and doesn't reply.

"The more the merrier," Bec says. She linked arms with Jess's. "Come on, grumpy. Let's see if I can still beat you at Ludo."

Chapter 22

A short time later Karin is relaxing on chaise lounge by the window while her friends battle it out over a game of chess on a rosewood table in front of a floor-to-ceiling bookcase with its own slide-along ladder. Bec's approach to is chess is simple. Kill off the enemy and the last one standing wins. The marble figurines fall quickly and *not fairs* fly from both sides of the table.

Karin blocks out her friends' squabbling and lets her gaze wander over the leather-bound books and neat family portraits hanging from the library's timber paneled walls.

And then she sees it. Propped on a table in the corner of the room, half-hidden behind velvet draped curtains, is the same photograph of their parents that Nev had given her. She stands and moves to the picture.

She hesitates, then picks it up and runs her fingers over the gilt-edged frame. "I think I just found where Nev got the photo of our parents."

Jess follows her gaze. "I wondered why it was familiar. It's odd that it's hidden away in the corner like that."

"Checkmate." Bec lays down Jess's king and extends her hand. "Let's go look at a dusty old photo of you parents and then move on to the portraits of the Maskell patriarchy glaring down at us like we're in Dumbledore's office in a Harry Potter movie.

She drags Jess to her feet, drags her to where Karin is standing and pulls her phone from the pocket of her cocktail dress. "Let's take one for the matriarchy. Smile, Jess. Let's show these stuffy old goats that their wall-hanging days are numbered."

"I was hoping to be remembered for something other than my looks," Jess says. "But here goes. How about this?" Jess drops her head forward and frees her hair from its constraining bun, runs her fingers through the long tresses, then flips her head back and pokes out her tongue.

Karin air-quotes a headline. "Thoroughly modern matriarch, Lady Jessalyn Maskell-Caddel, takes on the patriarchy on library wall."

Bec snaps the photo. "Immortalized at the ripe old age of thirty."

"The latest Maskell to go down in the history books as having lived unhappily ever after in isolated majesty." Jess adds an eyeroll to her tongue poke.

"Taking one for Team Maskell." Bec snaps another photo. "This time with crazy hair."

"But at least my babies will know I fought the good fight, at least for a while. Not like my darling Mumsie who spends her life flicking through online catalogues and flying in ice-carved dinner centrepieces."

"Actually, I thought they were kind of cool." Bec drops her phone back into her pocket, "I think your Mum has a cool life. She is Queen of all she surveys, which is how many thousands of acres? And I bet she has more than a little sway in your dad's decisions."

Jess laughs mercilessly and looks over as the door opens and Jess's mother enters with the silver tray with Dresden china cups and saucers, and matching milk jug and sugar bowl.

"Is that how it works, Mumsie? Are you the influencer in Dad's deals. The pillow talk to his boardroom machinations?"

Julia Maskell hesitates in the doorway, a slight frown marring her features. "Should I turn around and leave again? I was hoping for cosy women-gossip. I get enough aggression when you're not around."

"Ignore your daughter," Bec moves and takes the tray from the older woman. "She's worried about given up her freedom to immeasurable luxury and unimaginable wealth. Last hurrah jitters and all that."

Julia relaxes her and heads towards her daughter. "Come sit with me and tell me more about this freedom thing you're worried about. I'm sure that between us all we can come up with a solution."

Bec places the tray on the sideboard. "See, girls rule. Just what we were talking about." She moves to the liquor cabinet. "You don't mind if we have something stronger, do you Mrs Maskell. Like top shelf cognac. Courvoisier perhaps?"

"Whatever you want, Bec, darling. It's all there." She waves a hand at the liquor cabinet and turns to her daughter. "It's not such a bad life, you know. Married to the right man, you will have all the freedom you desire."

"Times have changed," Jess replies. "We want more. I've already got more. And I don't want to give it up."

"Who said anything about giving anything up? You will have more say than you do now. Your father is going to retire. Grayson will step up and you will be his partner. I don't know where you get the idea that marriage is about giving anything up."

"Oh, I don't know. Maybe watching you all these years."

"That's not fair." Julia's eyes are sparking fire.

Karin realises all they have done is bought time. Because the volcano they'd stopped from erupting at the dinner table is about to explode right here and now in the library.

"I suggest a truce," Bec says, amusement in her voice. "Jess, you already run your own business. You make your own decisions. You are more than capable of holding your own in any boardroom. Why the sudden doubts?"

"I think I can answer that one," Julia says, her eyes on a daughter as Jess resolutely turns her back to her mother. "When I married Jess's father everything I owned went into his name." She shrugs. "There is no secret that he married me for my money to prop this place up. There hasn't always been money in cattle farming, you know. And I'm guessing Jess is feeling the same way. That she's being pawned out to the highest bidder, the man who most benefits her father's business dealings. Am I right?"

Karin eyes Jess's rigid back and looks frantically at Bec. But she, too, is staring helplessly at their friend.

Jess turns around at spears her mother with a look that is at once both accusing and helpless. "You know that's exactly what's happening."

Julia places her cup carefully back on its saucer. "Only if you let it."

"What choice do I have?"

Jess's mother takes her daughter's hand and pulls her gently down onto the leather couch. "You can walk away," she says softly.

"You didn't."

"Back in my day we married who we were told to marry, and we made the most of what we had. Bloom where we were planted was drilled into our finishing school ethos. But that's not how things are any more. You have choices. And I fully support whatever choices you make. But I thought you love Grayson. I thought you were marrying him for the right reasons."

"So did I," Jess says. "Until he handed me the prenup."

Bec bursts out laughing. "I thought those things only happen in movies."

Karin shakes her head at her friend. *Not helping.*

But Bec is too fascinated to be circumspect. "You're for real, aren't you? Grayson's tying you up like a package that if he doesn't like he can mark return to sender. He rakes in the billions and you breed his babies. What happens if you don't have babies, Jess? Do you get beheaded, like in *Six?*"

Karin cups her head in her hands and waits for the explosion.

When there is none forthcoming, she looks over at the mother and daughter. Julia's arms are around her daughter and Jess's head is resting on her mother's shoulder. Both women are looking at Bec, and they are wearing identical smiles that are at once sad and defiant.

Bec's mouth drops open. "Oh no."

Jess straightens. "Oh yes."

Bec squeals and rushes over to Jess's other side. "You're pregnant. You're going to have a fucking baby. Which means all the carry-on is nothing but hormones." She laughs. "Toby is going to be over the moon. He will be an uncle. And you will have everything you ever dreamed of at your feet. All because you're carrying the future heir to the family fortune. Do we know if it's a boy or a girl yet? I suppose it doesn't matter. Look at you and Grayson. Talk about luck of the draw." Bec finally notices that her exuberance is falling flat and she falters to a stop.

Karin takes in the tableau and is at a loss for words. *Freedom to choose. Yeah, sure.* Jess's happily-ever-after just got real. And even if Bec can't see it, Karin knows how Jess's story will pan out. She can see in Jess's eyes, that she knows, too. Her story is already written. And that walking away is not an option.

It is Julia who takes control. "You haven't told your friends, have you?" Julia looks over Jess's head at Karin and Bec. "Roland doesn't want to make the announcement until after the wedding. Wants the focus on the happy couple and their nuptials. And I went along with it because I thought it would make my daughter's life easier. But I now realise how wrong I've been. Jessalyn, if you want to call off the wedding I'll support you. But if you want to go ahead with the wedding, we'll insist your father tears up the prenup."

Karin watches as Julia Maskell swings into action. She is surprised. To think that she thought the woman was unhappy, a victim of her circumstances. Something tells her that nothing about Julia's life is an accident. That like Karin's mother in the city, Julia has crafted exactly the life she wants.

She thinks again about photograph that has turned up twice now. Three women; one dead and the other two are masters of disguise.

The question is what are they hiding?

And from whom?

Karin is sick of fighting dead ends and leads that go nowhere. Maybe she has been looking in the wrong places. Her gaze is contemplative as she watches Julia Maskell comfort her daughter.

As she hugs her friends goodnight and air-kisses Julia Maskell's cheeks Karin begins to formulate a new plan. Not to find out about how her father was killed or even why, but what happened in the years before that, where four friends who went to university together and were so that close that they held annual reunions, no longer mention her parents' names.

Chapter 23

BACK in her room Karin showers and changes into a soft pink T-shirt that hangs to mid-thigh. She scrubs face, pulls her hair up in a band and cleans her teeth. What a night. She is glad that it is over.

She climbs into the wide fourposter bed and checks her phone. There is a missed call from Marshall. She checks her watch. He will still be awake.

"Hey, Marsh. You got something for me?"

"The picture you sent through. You are right that one of the men is Senator Flint. But you're wrong about who is standing next to him."

"Not his wife?"

"Not if the entry in the Australian Dictionary of Biography is correct. He is married to a Law Professor at the University of Western Australia. They have three boys. And even if I go back to their wedding photos the woman looks nothing like the woman in your photo."

Karin frowns. "Did the name Damascus Rose come up in your search?"

"That's where things get interesting. There's nothing in any records that I can find. I had to dig deeper."

"Let me guess. Our Senator is polyamorous."

Marsh chuckles. "If only it were that simple," he says. "By the way, you owe me. It took me all afternoon to find out what I'm about to tell you."

"You've got me intrigued. What could possibly be buried so deep that your brilliant mind couldn't find it."

"I found it, but it wasn't where you told me to look."

"Marshall Hennessy, if you don't tell me what's going on right now, I'll come down through the telephone line and pinch your nose. "

"There used to be a company listed on the stock exchange back in the day called Blue Sky? Heard of it?"

"I remember something about it. Didn't it go bust a few years ago after suffering a hit from short selling and dodgy reporting."

"That's part of it. There was also a subsidiary company called also Blue Skies Alternative Access. Blue Sky started with 33 million. In the next ten years, its earning assets grew to 3.4 billion. Before it all collapsed."

Karin frowns. The scandal was before her time, but she has heard mention of it. "And?"

He is enjoying the drama. "Well, it got me thinking—"

"Get on with the story, Hennessy. I need my beauty sleep."

"You of all people should appreciate the key to a good story is getting all your facts in order."

He has her there. She hasn't been able to line up the facts in her father's case. An untimely death. An accident at the railway. New technology. Kept under wraps. Until suddenly it's worth billions.

And after tonight, she can add the fact that two of the women in the photo have been hiding their true personalities for the last twenty years.

"That's what you're going to tell me, aren't you? The woman in the photograph. She was some rich investor dabbling in a little technology Company in the Pilbara when suddenly it blows out of all proportions and everybody makes a squillion. Except she is now dead and so is my father."

"Close, but no cookie."

She frowns again. "You don't mean—"

"I do mean. The woman in the picture, who you and your mother called Damascus Rose, was Damascus Rose Caddel who, it turns out, inherited part of the Caddel family fortune when her Texas magnate father died. Her brother, Holden, the other man in the photograph, co-inherited the Caddel fortune. And because the Senator and Rose were married at the time of her death, guess who inherited her share."

"Not her brother, I bet."

"You bet right. Brandon Flint inherited all his wife's goods and chattels a long time before he was a senator. But the brother, Holden, held the controlling share of the fortune."

"But surely a story like that would be all over the news. So why didn't I find anything when I went looking? A story like that should have been all over the front pages."

"Exactly. But you don't think I let a small detail like that stop me, do you?"

Karin can hear that her friend is enjoying himself but has been a long day and she is getting impatient. "Cut to the chase, Hennessy"

"It was in the early days of the Senator's political career. He was still in local politics in Perth, but he had political ambitions. And a dead wife wasn't in his best interests, especially an American heiress high on drugs who thought she could fly."

"He used his influence to cover up his wife's death." Karin sits up straighter in the bed. "And my father knew it."

"I'm guessing everyone in that photograph knew."

The enormity of what he is telling her finally sinks in. "My mother?"

"It would explain why she hasn't spent the money. Money gained by the death of another woman."

"And the investment in Dad's auto haul technology?"

"Does Damascus Holdings ring a bell? The Company benefited big time from the automation of over eight hundred kilometres of rail lines in the Pilbara that now carries over 400 million tons of ore a day to the Port of Dampier where it shipped across oceans far and wide. Think of the royalties," he says softly. "And think what would happen if I what I just told you became public knowledge."

"Old Nev was on the right track. He was trying to warn me, wasn't he?"

"It seems that way."

"Is there anything else I need to know or can I go to sleep."

"There's more, but it can wait if you want your beauty sleep."

"Like I'll sleep now," she says wryly, propping her back with pillows. "You might as well keep the good news rolling."

"There was a capitalisation around the time your father died, 2009. Hedge funds raise capital all the time. But it's unusual for an investor to stage a controlled buyout of a company's debts and take on a controlling interest of the company."

"Let me guess, Damascus Holdings bought out the debt."

"Your guess is correct. Roland Maskell and Brandon Flint of Damascus Holdings, and Holden Caddel, owner of the international shipping Company, Starr Shipping, who also happens to hold the contracts for the Dampier and Cape Lambert ports to run shiploads of Pilbara ore to steel plants in Japan and America."

"Was there ever any record of my father's name in any of the companies?"

"Not since before the auto-haul technology was released to shareholders."

"The bastards cut him out and paid my mother thirty million in hush money."

"Something like that. Hedge Funds raise capital, and the Headquarters of Damascus Holdings is offshore. I searched and filtered through the investor databases till I found what I was looking for. Starr capital. High yield and distressed credits debts. The portfolio made up of for strategies credit, private equity, re-real assets in listed equities. But Kaz, there's something else I need to tell you."

Karin shakes her head, trying to keep up with his rapid-fire revelations. "Don't tell me there are more heiresses out there."

"What did you say the name of your father's family property was?

"Mulga Plains."

"That's what I thought. Mulga Plains Station is part of a pastoral company who also own a pile of mining leases purchased around Mulga Plains. It looks like your father sold the family station to raise capital for his new technology."

"That he never got to profit from. Do we know who owns the pastoral company that sucked Mulga Plains into its jaws?"

"We do now."

"Let me guess. Damascus Holdings."

"'fraid so."

Karin remembers her uncle's warning. "Do you think Uncle Bernie knew who Dad sold out to?"

"It's usual for the oldest son to inherit, so your father could do what he wanted with Mulga Plains. But your uncle would have asked questions."

"Nev told me to follow the money. What he forgot to tell me was to work backwards. Marsh, you're a genius."

"Something tells me that the death of the Senator's wife is what started all the trouble. Tread carefully. Word on the ground is Damascus is trying to hedge funds, and the market is going against them."

"Do they stand to lose a lot of money? I hope they lose the lot."

"They'll be fine if they hold their positions but it's starting to look like someone is pulling the veritable rug out from under them. And Karin, there's something else you need to know. I heard whispers that you're undercover on a big story."

"What do you mean, undercover? I walked away, Marsh. I needed a break."

"You and I know that, but it seems that some think otherwise. I may have called in a few favours while I was digging, and your name may have come up in the same sentence as potential asset selloffs in the Pilbara."

"And that means?"

"Someone is getting ready to move one of three things around: credit, equity, or assets. And there is only one reason to do that."

"Covering their tracks."

"Blue sky was a huge success story until it wasn't. The same could happen to Damascus Holdings. If even a whiff of what I told you gets out and the short sellers move in, your Senator and your friend's father both stand to lose a bucketload."

Karin thinks of old Nev's warning. "I'll be careful," she promises.

"Do that," he replies. "And if I hear anything I'll keep you posted."

"Thanks, Marsh, I owe you." Karin ends the call.

What is she supposed to do now?

Chapter 24

Sleep eludes her. The dinner, Jess's news and Julia Maskell's determination to protect her daughter, and Marsh's revelations about the Maskell's finances are all jostling in her brain for attention. But she is too tired to make sense of any of it.

Instinctively, she reaches for Trouble and realises she has no idea where he is, or even if he has been fed. Of course, Julia Maskell would not allow a dog on her eight hundred thread linen. And for all Karin knows, her poor pooch has been relegated to the stables.

What kind of mother is she that she has neglected the wellbeing of her dog? She shoots off a text to the one person she can trust in a crisis, hoping that Lukah is not asleep.

You awake?

Nope

I've lost my dog

And you're telling me because—

Because we've got to go find him

Okay, you have my attention. First, tell me what you're wearing

What's that got to with my dog—

Want to know what I'm wearing?

No

Chica, you're really bad at sexting

Sexting? My dog could be getting torn apart by a dingo and your brain is in your pyjama bottoms?

I didn't pack jarmies

No dirty talk. This is serious

Want me to come comfort you?

Lukah, behave yourself

Oh okay. He's with Toby. When I checked on the them they were both fast asleep

You checked on my dog?

I checked on you first but you were in the middle of a girl-crisis so I had time on my hands

Jess is pregnant and Mr Maskell is insisting on a pre-nup and—

The phone buzzes mid-tex. Karin hits answer. "I haven't finished my message—"

"And you haven't told me what you're wearing."

"I don't do phone sex either."

"Damn. It was worth a try."

"Thank you for checking on my dog."

"No worries."

She hears the rustle of sheets and imagines him pulling himself upright, his chest bare—and other parts—she scrambles to redirect her thoughts. "Marsh called when I came back to my room."

There is a moment's silence as Lukah regroups. "And?"

"We know Dad sold Mulga Downs to Damascus Holdings and Marsh confirmed the names behind that company." She settles more comfortably against her pillows and waits while he mulls over her statement.

It doesn't take him long. "He was screwed over by none other than our illustrious host."

"Correct. Along with his other longtime friend, Senator Brandon Flint."

"And the third man in the photograph. Good guy or bad?"

"Holden Caddel. American shipping magnate. He didn't go to university with the others like we thought. He was in the photo for a different reason."

"American? He's our link with your father's overseas trips."

"Yep. But it gets better. His sister, Damascus Rose Caddel, was an heiress to a Texas mining magnate. And guess who inherited her fortune?"

"Our good Senator, maybe?"

"You're no fun. Bet I can tell you something you don't know."

There is an unmistakable leer in his tone. "Is there a prize?"

"Depends." Karin smiles, a challenge in her voice. "If you can fly."

The silence on the end of the phone is so drawn-out Karin wonders if he has fallen asleep. "Something tells me I don't want to ask what you mean by that."

"We need to fly to Dampier." She pauses. "Tomorrow, first thing."

Lukah's groan is audible. "Please tell me we're not going to commandeer Jess's chopper without her permission."

"Okay, I won't tell you. And now that we've got business out of the way, I'm ready to be introduced to the pleasures of phone sex."

"You want phone sex after telling an officer of the law he needs to commit a felony to curry your favours?"

She is laughing now. "I thought it might ease your tension."

"Tension?"

"Yeah. You know, help you sleep so we can get an early start in the morning."

"Something tells me I won't be getting much sleep either way. And due to your criminal tendencies, I seem to have lost the urge for anything even remotely romantic. How about you tell me what you girls were up to in the library, while I was doing a welfare check on your dog?"

She had forgotten about her half-written text. "Jess is having wedding jitters."

"Poor old Grayson. Does he know his fiancée is having doubts?"

"She says he's having the same doubts. Neither of them like being manipulated by their families." She wonders briefly if breaking Jess's confidence is the right thing to do—but she is asking him to steal a helicopter for her. The least she can do is trust him. "There's one more thing. Jess is pregnant."

She can tell by his silence that Lukah is shocked. "Does Grayson know?"

"I'm not sure. Jess's father does. It's his idea to keep the pregnancy under wraps till after the wedding. And he's insisting on a prenup."

"Sounds like a marriage made in heaven. I can almost see why you're gun shy."

"I don't need a piece of paper to tie me to any man," she says. "But I'll take any good bits you have to offer."

"What good bit are we talking about? Is this where we resume our phone sex?"

She laughs and sinks into her pillows. "We could always Facetime so I can stop imagining your chest and actually see it."

"Deal. You want me to hang up and call you back or do you want to take the lead?"

"On second thought, think I can contain my lust for you in check until tomorrow."

"I'll see you bright and early. Unless you change your mind and I don't have to indulge in criminal activity to impress you."

"I'm already impressed. After all this is over, you'll have to tell me about any other skills you possess that I don't know about."

"Oh, darlin', you've got no idea what you're asking. I suggest you end this call before I change my mind and show you exactly what skills I have that you're missing out on."

"And I you. Goodnight, Lukah." She is smiling as she ends the call.

As she sets an alarm and places her phone on the bedside cabinet, she lays back on her pillows and finishes her phone sex fantasy with Lukah in her mind.

Chapter 25

THE new day is starting to lighten the sky as Karin makes her way to the station's hangar. The sun is yet to break the horizon, but already she can feel the heat. "Are you sure you know how to fly?"

"I was hoping you'd changed your mind." Lukah pauses mid-stride. "You know stealing is a criminal offence, right?"

She grins. "We're not stealing it. We're borrowing it. Besides, I texted Jess and asked her." She doesn't mention that she sent the text in the middle of the night and that Jess would still be fast asleep long after they are halfway to the coast.

Lukah looks at her suspiciously. "Where exactly are we headed for this joyride of yours?"

"Dampier," she says promptly. "Just follow the railway lines if your navigation skills are rusty."

His gaze narrows on her face. "You've been checking up on me to see if I can really fly this baby, haven't you?"

"I had to do something last night after you got me all hot and bothered." She is openly laughing at him now and wonders how much she will regret it when he finally gets her somewhere private and alone.

"You hacked into the Civil Aviation Safety Authority website?"

"Hack is such an ugly word. No. I have a friend—"

He holds up a hand. "Spare me the details. I don't want to store any more criminal knowledge than I need to in case they torture me afterwards."

Karin is about to reply in kind when she hears a scraping sound coming from the hangar. She turns her gaze to the silver double doors, which are being shoved open from the inside.

"About time you guys got here," a voice calls from the other side of the doors. "We've been waiting for ages."

Karin peers into the darkened hangar and spots Jess dropping the bolt to hold one side of the doors open. Her gaze shoots to the other side, where Grayson is bolting the other door open. "Did you pair sleep out here?"

Jess laughs. "We may have. Grayson suggested...you know...and I thought why not. And here we are."

Grayson looks sheepish. "Camping out under the stars with my fiancée seemed like good idea, all things considered." He glances at Karin. "And it was working, until her phone went off."

Grayson just went up a notch in Karin's esteem. He had his fiancée's back when all hell was breaking loose around them. "Remind me never to underestimate you. And sorry about the middle-of-the-night text."

He nods and takes Jess's hand before eyeing Lukah. "If you're up to flying this baby, then we're taking the back seat. We need to sleep off all that stargazing."

"Looks like you're it," Jess says, punching Lukah lightly on the shoulder. "I hope you remember everything I taught you, because I'm with him." She leans into Grayson's embrace and the pair walk back into to the shed and climb into the chopper.

Karin watches helplessly as they lean their heads against each other and promptly fall asleep. Lukah hitches the tractor to the dolly and tows the chopper out the helipad while Karin closes the shed doors and follows him. She hauls herself into the front passenger seat and puts her headset on. Lukah does a visual check around the outside of the chopper and then he swings himself lightly aboard. He pulls on his headset and runs through the pre-flight checklist attached to the control column.

He smiles over at her, his voice in her ear. "You okay?"

Note to self: *Bec can have the front seat on the way home from the station.* "Fine."

"When she says fine, she really means she's scared shitless," Jess joined in from the back seat.

So much for being asleep in her lover's arms. Traitor. "I'm not scared shitless. Not even."

"I bet her eyes are closed," Jess said.

She feels Lukah's hand rest on her knee, his voice calm and quiet through her headset. "You'll be okay. Trust me."

She nods, and the sound of his voice distracts her from her fear, replacing it with something more dangerous. Lust. She reminds herself she is immune to the charms of handsome policeman sitting next to her with his hand resting lightly on her knee.

She keeps reminding herself for the next half-hour as they follow the mountains to the coast.

By the time the deep blue of the Dampier Archipelago comes into view, she is more than ready to escape the confines of the chopper, and the heat emanating between them that has nothing to do with the rising Pilbara sun.

"We need to hire a vehicle and make our way to the Seven Mile," she instructs.

"We're in Karratha?" Jess is awake in the back seat and peering down at the airport surrounded by salt flats. "I was hoping we were going somewhere a little more interesting, like Millstream Falls."

"Sorry. You're out of luck," Lukah replies as he brings the chopper down onto the waiting helipad with a gentle hand. "Karin is sleuthing, and we're just along for the ride."

"Maybe we can steal a yacht," Jess says sleepily to Grayson. "And sail off into the wide blue yonder."

Grayson chuckles. "A deserted island. Great idea. How many of them are there to choose from again?"

"Forty-two."

"Let's do it. Actually, I already own a yacht moored at the marina, which will save us having to steal one. Unless you think it would be more fun to—"

"Children," Lukah warns. "Officer of the law listening."

"Oh, yeah. Sorry, forgot."

Did Grayson Caddel just snigger? Karin turns around to stare at the affianced couple, who look back at her with innocent eyes. She doesn't trust them a bit. What is wrong with them? They are acting like lovesick teenagers. Whatever had happened out under the stars last night appears to be just what Jess needed. The lines of worry are gone from around her eyes, replaced by what Karin can only describe as mischief. Karin is not sure which is worse, and makes a mental note to consult with Bec at the first opportunity.

"I also have a vehicle on standby," Grayson adds. "Save you mucking around with a hire car."

A short time later, Karin finds herself in the front seat of Grayson's Range Rover as they exit the airport on Bailey Avenue and turning right towards the Dampier Peninsula. "Where exactly are we headed?"

"To Parker Point at the port. Follow the signs to Burrup Peninsula."

Karin watches the scalloping powerlines dip and sway above the salt flats as Lukah guides the vehicle across the causeway to Dampier, where the port dominates the skyline. Railway tracks drill lines parallel to the road, busy with ore trains spilling their loads via conveyor belts into the huge tankers docked at Parker Point and East Intercourse Island terminals.

Karin counts three tankers as she scans the docks, with their busloads of workers, carparks guarded by boom gates, and dock vehicles with their flashing lights. The industrial precinct is dotted with a plethora of *Keep Out, No Unauthorised Vehicles,* and *Danger* signs. Kilometres of two-metre-high chain wire fencing line the roadways, interspersed with padlocked gates and gatehouses with security guards and manifests.

The harbour is busy with tugboats, security vessels and the looming presence of the bulk carriers with their jaws open, sucking tens of thousands of tonnes of ore into their bowels. Once loaded, the carriers will wend their way to the open ocean and empty carriers, waiting at anchor, will take their place.

The docks are a twenty-four-seven operation, much bigger than Karin expected, and she is not sure where to go or what to do now that she has dragged them all here.

"Should we turn back and head to Dampier to grab something to eat?" Lukah pulls the vehicle over at yet another *No Public Access* dead-end cul-de-sac and eyes her with concern.

She rests her head on the headrest and looks at the roof of the vehicle as if inspiration is lurking there. And sighs. She turns and looks at the man at her side. He hasn't questioned her sanity, but his concern is telling. "We need to find a shipping office, but I have no idea where to look," she admits.

There is a noise from the back seat that sounds a lot like a chuckle, and suddenly Grayson is leaning forward between them. "Remind me. What are we doing here again?"

Lukah shrugs. "No idea, mate." He stares at the harbour visible through the chain wire fencing. "Playing tourists, maybe."

Grayson turns to Karin. "Is it secret women's business? Tell me if I'm crossing a line, but maybe I can help."

"I'm looking for a shipping company." Karin rubs her hands over her face. "I know the trains deliver ore to the port, but I'm not sure what happens after that." *And who profits.* But she's not saying that part out loud. "I was just curious, that's all."

"Do you have a name?"

Karin hesitates. But it's either tell him why they are here or admit she has dragged them all on a wild goose chase. "Starr Shipping."

"Easy. See the Toll Dampier Supply Base over there?" Karin follows the direction he is pointing. "Next door is what you're looking for, and as luck would have it, I brought my security pass with me."

Grayson disappears into the back seat and in his place dangles a lanyard with a plastic card. "There you go, mate. Wave that in front of the security post and you'll get through without question."

Lukah does what he says and pulls the vehicle up in front of a non-descript shed with a discreet logo on its side: *Starr Shipping, Global Carriers.*

"If it's any help, we've been chartering for the mining companies since the nineties. My uncle flew in from the States last week and I believe he's around here somewhere. If I'd known we were coming, I would have organised a guided tour. Sorry."

Karin is out of the car and heading to the office, not waiting to see if the others follow. She pushes open the door and pauses. There is nobody at the counter, but there is a logo on the wall telling her she is in the right place. A plant sits on the counter beside a bowl of mints and a holder filled with business cards. There is a computer with a wraparound screen on the desk behind the counter, and a door with one-way mirrored glass and a security pad leading off to another room.

Karin walks over to the counter. There is no buzzer to advise of their arrival. As she waits, the others file in behind her. Jess fans herself and drops onto a leather lounge under a window overlooking the bay.

Grayson heads to the watercooler, pours a cup of water and takes it to his fiancée. Caretaking done, he walks over to where Karin is standing. "If I'd known you were interested in Starr Shipping, maybe I could have saved your trip."

Karin stills. "What you mean?"

Lukah, who has come to stand beside Karin, looks between the two of them in confusion but says nothing, waiting and watching like he is not sure whether Karin needs to be protected or taken in for questioning like some crazy bag lady.

"Holden is my uncle. Well, a distant one. One of our British ancestors married a dollar princess, which is a fancy term for an American heiress. When Holden turned up on our doorstep with grand ideas to expand the family shipping empire, Father not only adopted him but introduced him to the right people. Starr is now the leading carrier for the mining companies shipping ore to far-flung countries, and makes a nice profit doing it."

Karin starts to laugh softly, but hysteria is not far away. She leans against Lukah, unable to formulate the words to make the situation more surreal than it already is. She doesn't dare turn and look at his face.

"I don't believe it." Karin feels Lukah's arm snake around her waist, and she is hauled against his side. "We got up with the sparrows, risked life and limb with me in the cockpit of a chopper that may or may not have been purloined without permission, and gave up a day of luxuriating around the pool watching my girlfriend in a bikini, all for no reason?"

Karin can't contain her laughter another minute. She collapses against him, her body shaking. "I'll make it up to you, promise."

"You'd better." He leans down, his words for her ears only. "Starting with where we left off last night."

But Karin is no longer listening. "The money." *Follow the money.* Marsh had spelled it out for her last night, and she had been too tired to see it. Too distracted by other things. *Admit it. Like sex talk with a handsome policeman. Who had just called her his girlfriend.* She pulls out of Lukah's arms and turns to Grayson.

And that's when she sees the photograph. She stares over the counter at the wall with its Starr Shipping logo. Beside it is a sepia photograph of four men, their arms over each other's shoulders, and they are laughing at the camera like they know a secret the rest of the world is yet to figure out. It's the same photo Nev had given her on the USB.

Karin is mesmerised as she stares at the photograph. Here, in the shipping office, so much is starting to make sense. The dead ends. The gaps in her research. The silence. And the cover-up of her father's death. The men in the photograph have so much more to lose than the auto-haul technology.

"Your uncle was my father's friend. Did you know that?"

Grayson nods, his eyes sympathetic as he meets her gaze. "I heard about the accident. I was away at university at the time."

Karin straightens and steps away from Lukah, her gaze not leaving Grayson's face. "I think your uncle is the money behind Damascus Holdings, the company set up after my father's death and used to launder the funds from his auto-haul technology. I don't suppose you know how they came up with the name of the company?"

Grayson frowns. "My father told me it was in honour of Uncle Holden's sister who had passed away."

It is the connection Karin has been missing. Holden and Rose Caddel, brother and sister. Arrived from America to expand their family business. But nowhere in her research had Karin made the connection to Grayson's family, Pilbara pastoralists for generations, and the same ilk as the Maskells.

Full circle. Her father had never been in the same league, but she could see how he dreamt he might be one day. What had Uncle Bernie told her? That her father had sold out. Maybe he was right, after all.

"Any other family secrets we need to know about?" Jess says from her chair. She is sipping her water, feigning mild interest, but her eyes are sharp.

Grayson holds up his hands. "Don't shoot me for my relatives." He stares more closely at the photograph and turns to Karin. "I'm sorry. I didn't make the connection before you pointed it out just now."

Karin sees that he is genuine and she almost feels sorry for him, except there is more she needs from him. "No worries. It means I don't have to tear this place apart to get access to the deets about share prices and shipping routes for the last ten years." She widens her eyes, her expression innocent. "Because all I have to do is ask you to dig them out for me."

"I don't know about that," a new voice joins in, and Karin finds herself looking into the eyes of an older version of one of the men in the photograph. "He would have to ask me, and I might say no." He extends his hand to Karin. "Holden Caddel. I was a friend of your father's. He was a good man."

Karin ignores his hand and meets his gaze with a steely look of her own. "Is there any reason that you would say no?"

His smile tightens.

Karin swallows her satisfaction as his gaze locks with hers. *Glad I've got your attention. And you might as well tell me what you're hiding, because I'm going to find out anyway.* She does not say the words aloud, but the narrowing of his gaze tells her that he gets her message and he doesn't like it.

Grayson steps between them. "Hi, Unc. Didn't know you had arrived in the country already."

Holden breaks eye contact with Karin and turns to his nephew. "I heard there was a rather special wedding to attend, so I thought I'd kill two birds with one stone. I flew in early to take care of business." His gaze flicks to Jess. "Then I'm heading out to the Windclema for a bit of rest and relaxation before the big day. I thought you young ones were there already. What are you doing in Dampier when you could be around the pool enjoying Julia's hospitality?"

His words are benign, but his gaze returns to Karin.

She steps forward. "They're here because of me. I had questions that needed answering and I thought here was a good place to start. And Grayson offered to help."

Until you turned up.

The older man is sizing her up. Wondering how much she knows and how much to give away. And like Roland Maskell at dinner, he is shrewd enough not to underestimate her.

"You're just like him," he said. "You father was straight to the point." *And look what happened to him.*

"My father trusted you. I know that much. Don't expect me to make the same mistake."

His gaze flattens. "I'm not sure we should be having this conversation in front of your friends and my nephew—"

Lukah steps in front of Karin, his hand outstretched. "Morning, Sir. Lukah Sorreli, local copper out at Nameless. And pilot for our jaunt to the coast. Apologies for not ringing ahead."

"Grayson speaks highly of you all." Holden's voice is cordial as he shakes Lukah's hand. "And you weren't to know I'd be here. Apology accepted."

Karin shoots a look at look at Lukah. *Back off, buddy. This is my party.* She holds up her phone to the older man. "Do you know this man, Senator Brandon Flint?"

He chuckles. "What you expect me to say? We're standing together in the photograph behind you on the wall. Slightly younger versions of us, that is. We all went to university together."

"And your sister, Rose. Was it you who introduced her to the Senator?"

The hiss of his breath gives her no satisfaction. "I think we need to talk. But now is not the time." His smile is pointed before he turns away, his gaze coming to rest on Jess—who is staring back at him, her face deliberately expressionless until she crushes her plastic cup in her hand and stands.

"You said you were coming out to the Windelema. Maybe this conversation can wait until my father is around, and then you can both regale us with your stories from the *good old days*."

The emphasis of her words is not lost on any of them.

Karin smiles. Jess isn't her mother's daughter for nothing. It sounds like she is being genial, but that's not what her friend is doing at all. She is telling them how things will unfold. In her time, at her pleasure. Julia Maskell would be proud of her daughter.

Holden inclines his head. "I'll leave you to it then." He turns to his nephew. "I'll finish up here and then I'll take the light plane out to the Windelema. You can help me out here, or you can go with your friends."

Grayson reaches for Jess's hand. "Actually, we think we might take the chopper for a bit. Unc, would mind dropping Karin and Lukah back at the station for us?"

Karin turns to stare at him, her mouth open. She closes it again with a snap, trying valiantly to hold back the laugh rising deep in her belly. Jess and Grayson weren't along for the ride this morning. They were doing a runner. Aided and abetted by the local constabulary, who at this moment is looking like a giant ball of guilt wrapped in a sexy-as-hell covering, like he knows he is going to pay big time for his deception, and he is looking forward to his punishment.

The wicked gleam in Jess's eyes as she looks from Lukah to Karin cements her suspicion. She has been set up. Jess and Grayson had this planned all along, and their escape was always a foregone conclusion.

"We'll be back in time for dinner," Jess promises, poker faced. "I'm taking Grayson out to the Millstream to show him the local waterfalls."

Karin watches their retreating backs, admiring their audacity, and turns to Lukah, who shrugs and grins. "What can I say? Young love and all that. They made me do it."

"You can say—and do—plenty. But you're right. Now isn't the time or the place." She takes his hand and squeezes it—a promise that he will pay the price for lying to her, and that the price may be more than he bargained for. She turns and smiles at Grayson's uncle, the smile not reaching her eyes. "Looks like we're at your mercy, sir. We'll take a stroll and look at the ships until you're ready to go if that's okay."

Holden Caddel eyes her speculatively. "Sounds like a plan. Tell Security I've authorised you to look around. If you have any problems, get them to call me."

As he turns towards the back office, Karin has a feeling he is watching them through the reflective glass and weighing his chances that she is as good as her bravado makes out. Or whether she will let things drop for the sake of her friend's wedding. It is a question she can no more answer than he can. But one thing is certain: he will not make the mistake of underestimating the daughter of the man he and Roland Maskell have wronged.

And if he does, Karin will make sure he pays with every cent he ever stole and laundered through the company bearing his sister's name.

Chapter 26

HOLDEN lands the light plane on the tarmac at Windelema. The windsock hangs limply and even the heat is torpid. Karin's T-shirt slews against her body, the cotton material making contact like slush against her skin. She steps out onto the plane's wing and Lukah helps her down onto the tarmac.

Julia Maskell is sitting in the station's Land Rover on the edge of the runway. She is staring straight ahead and as Karin gets closer, she notices the woman's hands are gripping the steering wheel like she would rather be anywhere else than sitting on the tarmac in the heat of the day waiting for them to arrive.

Holden holds the back door open for Karin and Lukah, shuts it after them, and climbs into the front besides Julia.

He doesn't speak.

Karin finds herself looking at the back of Julia's head. She is staring resolutely forward, guiding the vehicle along a barely discernible track leading away from the homestead towards a low hill.

She brings the vehicle to a halt at the tree line of a dry riverbed. She leaves the car running and makes no effort to get out.

A straggle of hardy trees provide shade for a cluster of graves marked by headstones made from local stone. Karin gets out of the vehicle and walks towards the graves whose inscriptions are faded by the heat and wind and rains.

She fights down a shiver at the isolated beauty of the small cemetery. Lukah squeezes her hand and doesn't let go.

The cemetery holds four generations of the Maskell family and station hands. Karin can remember coming here with Jess and Bec.

The cemetery had held a macabre appeal. They had smoked their first cigarettes here and drunk their first stolen bottle of wine.

But Holden doesn't pause at the family graves. He walks past the cluster of Maskell gravestones, bidding Karin and Lukah to follow. And only when he reaches the crest does he stop and meet Karin's gaze.

At the back of the cemetery with a view of the sparse vegetation and rugged landscape, backdropped by the open country of the Pilbara plains, stands a single grave. It is stark in its isolation. Beautiful.

Karin frowns. "Your sister?"

"Correct. Buried but not forgotten. Never that." He looks out across rugged hills, almost as if he has forgotten Karin and Lukah are there. "Forever in my heart, my dearest. Just like I promised."

Karin kneels beside the gravestone and brushes her fingers over the weathered stone.

Damascus Rose Flint
Beloved wife of Brandon
Loved sister of Holden
May she rest in peace
Forever in our hearts
B. November 1961 D. September 2007

Karin stares at the grave. The woman they had been searching for has been here all along. She stands and looks at Holden, reading the grief, the distress, and the relief that the secret is finally out. That he can mourn his sister, knowing she is safe out here; from prying eyes, the whispers and the rumours of a life ended too soon in a place so far away that suspicions are buried with the questions about a woman who lived so large in everyone's hearts that each and every one who came in contact with the beauty that was Damascus Rose asked themselves was there anything they could have done to prevent the tragedy had they but known of her struggles. Or thought to ask the question in the first place.

Julia steps from the car and moves to stand beside Holden. She slips an arm around his waist and rests her head against his chest. "She's at peace here. We did the right thing."

"Did we? So much secrecy."

"Hush. Karin has the answers she needs." Julia shoots Karin a look that is both victorious and resigned. "You will let it go, won't you, Karin? The woman in the photograph is Rose Caddel. Her beautiful restless soul has found peace out here. I insist you let her continue to rest in peace. And allow the men to continue running Damascus Holdings in her memory without interference. It's time to let it go. For all our sakes. But mostly for the woman in front of you. She wouldn't have wanted the unhappiness to continue."

Julia stares at Karin for long moments as if she can force Karin to do her bidding by asserting her will. Is that how she has survived her marriage to Roland Maskell? Sheer bloody mindedness mixed with a lethal dose of control. No wonder Jess is feeling fragile. Going up against Julia Maskell is daunting enough. Having her as a mother is another whole level of manipulation. And for what? A family name and the prestige that goes with being one of the Pilbara's first families. But Karin has seen it unravel before. And she has a sinking feeling she is about to witness it again. Only this time, she will be the instigator, the one who takes them down, her father's friends, the men responsible for his death. Whether they were the ones who actually killed him or not. And her best friend will be caught in the fallout.

There is a reason she has kept her business and personal life separate all these years. Keeping her professional distance has allowed her to protect her heart. This time the truth will heal it.

But at what cost?

Karin watches as Julia takes Holden's hand and they head back the way they have come, leaving Karin staring helplessly at their backs. Coming home was a mistake. And it is too late to prevent the hurt that is bound to follow.

Lukah guides Karin back to the vehicle. She sinks into the coolness of the back seat, not bothering to pull a seatbelt on. Lukah reaches over and clips her in, and the gentle brush of his lips on her forehead reminding her she is not alone.

Julia guides the vehicle back to the homestead in silence. Karin stares out the window, lost in thought.

Such a fucking mess.

So many people's lives ruined.

And the secret, despite Julia's best efforts to squash it, is still alive to ruin a new generation.

It is why Nev has given her the USB. Jess's wedding. The old gang getting back together to celebrate their sins.

And it is eating at Nev's guts.

The men had put their self-interest ahead of a flamboyant independent woman and the best they could do was a grave in the middle of nowhere where no-one would know what had happened to her, except those involved.

But it wasn't just the men. Julia Maskell and her own mother were also guilty. Karin gazes at the back of Julia's head. The station wife. The dutiful wife. The wife who entertained her husband's guests with a style honed at her mother's knee.

While all the while she hated him.

Karin isn't sure if she would have the strength to do the same in her position.

But Julia has her own burden to carry with a daughter of her own to raise. Jess; wife, mother, and perfect hostess. Karin cannot imagine her best friend giving in to the life planned out for her. Because Jess is as independent as the woman buried on the hill with her eternal view of the Pilbara plains, the duty to her parents' wishes sitting heavily on her shoulders—

That's it. The piece of the puzzle that has refused to fit, and the reason Julia Maskell drove them to the cemetery and not her husband.

Jess is not Julia's daughter. She is the birth daughter of Damascus Rose. Karin closes her eyes to better arrange the pieces. Roland Maskell insisting on a prenup. The missing birth certificate. The strained relationship between the husband and wife. But the most damning proof is Jess herself. The woman who would rather elope than succumb the life mapped out for her parents. *Is that why you jumped, Damascus Rose, to escape the life mapped out for you by your husband? Did Brandon Flint's political aspirations suck the life out of you before you climbed the mountain?*

Nev had told Karin that first day the sins of the fathers were land, money and power. He knew he could never get close to the Senator and his secrets. But the bastard daughter of his best mate with the skillset of a trained investigative journalist had every chance in the world. He had Karin's guilt against her. By staying away so long she had been halfway to committing to finding out who killed her father the moment she had arrived in town. She just hadn't admitted it to herself

Karin stares silently out the window as Julia pulls the Land Rover into the circular driveway in front of the homestead. Lukah has his fingers linked loosely with hers but he, too, is silent. It is only when Julia kills the engine that Karin looks up. She is surprised to see Roland Maskell on the verandah, his arms crossed on the railing, staring out.

He straightens as the party alight from the vehicle, his gaze trained on his wife. "I've just been apprised of the fact that our daughter and her fiancée have eloped and that the wedding is cancelled."

Lukah draws Karin to his side, stilling her with a glance. He slips an arm around her waist, and she feels him tense. He shoots a questioning glance towards Holden who shakes his head imperceptibly.

It is Julia Maskell who breaks the tableau. She moves towards her husband and stops so close to him Karin barely hears the words she hurls at her husband. "You were the one who drew up the prenup. Did you really think our daughter would allow you to control the lives of her children the same way you have controlled her life? At least have the decency to lay the fault where it belongs."

She pushes past him and enters the house. Karin reads the shock in Roland Maskell's eyes before he has time to mask it. It is like his wife is a stranger who has forgotten her social cues and he is not sure whether to laugh it off or go after her and demand an apology.

His gaze skims over Karin and Lukah, and rests on his old friend. "Holden, good to see you. But I'm afraid your trip may prove to be for nothing if my daughter and your nephew continue to be irascible."

Holden moves forward and slings and arm over his old friend's shoulder. "Time will tell, I guess. In the meantime, I suggest we retire to your study and discuss our options."

The two men disappear in the same direction as Julia, leaving Karin and Lukah alone.

"Bit of a mess," Lukah says. "Do you suppose Jess and Grayson are serious about eloping?"

"I don't think even they know the answer to that question. They're operating on survival mode and that Grayson wanted to get Jess as far the hell away as he could."

"What do we do now?"

Karin is saved the effort of replying as Trouble races around the side of the homestead and launches himself at her. Toby is hard on his heels. They are both soaking wet like they have escaped the pool but only for the purpose of drenching Karin and Lukah before racing back the way they came.

"I don't know about you," Karin shakes the water off her as best she can. "But I think it's time for a swim."

"Sounds like as good an idea as any," Lukah agrees, his gaze sweeping the front of her T-shirt as he suppresses a smile.

They follow the dog and the boy around the side of the homestead, kick of their shoes and launch themselves into the pool where Toby is trying valiantly to hide behind Arno and Bec who up until this moment were floating on daybeds with cocktails.

When the chaos dies down, Karin surfaces to find Bec at her side and there is concern in her eyes. "Are you okay?"

"I think so." Karin raises her hands and runs her fingers through the tangles of her hair. "I think I truly am now that Jess is safe."

Chapter 27

ON THE way back to town Lukah drives with Karin at his side. The rest of their party are piled in the back, fast asleep.

Karin stares out the window, saying little.

"Penny for them?"

Karin turns and takes in his profile. "I understand why Jess and Grayson did what they did. "I'd do the same if it meant escaping all the craziness. Sometimes I'm glad Mum buried us away in the suburbs. Poor Jess has never had the opportunity of anonymity. And now a high-profile wedding with God knows what's at stake. Cancelled."

"I think we should run with the theory that you're reading too much into it. Let's get back to town. Get some sleep will get some rest I maybe things will be brighter. And hopefully Jess and Grayson will come to their senses and return for their wedding."

Karin leans back in the seat and closes her eyes. She had seen the stress in her friend's face, heard in her voice. She isn't surprised Jess had hightailed it with her fiancé. Nor did Grayson protectiveness surprise her. Who would have thought easy-going Grayson would stand up when it mattered?

She opens her eyes and sighs. "You're right. Drop me at the caravan park. Maybe we can get together later to the discuss wedding plans."

Bec yawns and stretches in the back seat. "We've decided there's going to be a wedding, after all? Have you heard from Jess?"

"None of the above." Karin turns back to look at her friend. "Just wishful thinking I guess."

"I don't know why they didn't get married out at the station," Bec says. "That place is amazing."

"I've got a theory on that," Lukah joins in. "What if some wayward guest found their way to the family cemetery and discovered Rose's grave. Wouldn't be a good look, would it."

They finish the journey in silence, Lukah dropping Bec, Arno and Toby first, then looking at Karin. "You sure you want to stay at the caravan park? My place is air-conditioned. And I'll be at work. You'll have the place to yourself."

Karin is tempted. "Okay, but can we swing past my van while I grab my things."

They drive in silence to the park.

Lukah pulls up beside her van. "Did you leave the van open?"

She shakes her head. "No."

"Stay in the car," he orders. But she is halfway out even as he pulls the car to a stop.

The van door is open and Karin sees her things scattered across the bed. Trouble jumps into the van and sniffs before turning soulful eyes to her.

Karin scratches his head. "It's okay, mate."

"Hold the dog," Karin orders. And enters the van.

Inside, the damage is superficial. She checks the cupboards, drawers and wardrobe, but nothing is missing. She looks around. Her laptop case is askew on the table. And the pocket stitching is ripped. She opens the case and runs her hand around inside the pocket. The USB is gone.

Lukah pokes his head inside. "What were they looking for?"

She hesitates, not sure how much to tell him.

"Don't even think it."

"The USB Nev gave me. It's gone." Her gaze narrows and she swivels to the glovebox in the front of the van. "Lukah, check the glove box. There should be an envelope."

Lukah rummages in the glove box. He extracts a crumpled envelope and holds it out to her. "This? It looks like a piece of rubbish.

I can see how someone would have missed it. You really need to tidy out the mess in there."

Karin ignores him and snatches the envelope. She smooths it out on the knee of her jeans. "Maybe it wasn't the USB they were looking for. Maybe it was this?"

Lukah looks from her to the envelope and back.

"The postmark," she says quietly. "When Nev gave me the USB it was inside this envelope. My guess is whoever sent Nev the photographs in the first place wanted them back."

"Whoever turned over your van wasn't looking for the USB."

"My bet is they wanted the envelope because the postmark is tell-tale sign who is behind this."

"Then Nev isn't in it on his own?"

"I don't think so. If he'd been worried about the envelope he wouldn't have given it to me in the first place. I think Nev knew the men in the photograph, including the Senator and his wife. And he wanted me to know so I could follow up on their financial dealings."

While she talks Lukah through her theory, she scrunches the envelope in her hand and shoves it into her pocket, hoping Lukah doesn't ask the question that is so obvious.

"Do we know anyone who lives in Floreat?"

Damn. "You had to ask. My uncle Bernie, the State Representative for the Mining Union"

"Grab your things. You're coming back to mine with me."

For once, Karin doesn't argue. She grabs things for her and Trouble, locks the van door, not that it had made any difference the first time.

She hunts Trouble into the back seat of Lukah's vehicle and climbs into the front, securing her seatbelt.

Lukah holds up his phone.

She looks at the screen. "Tyre tracks?"

He grins. "You're not the only detective around here. While you were searching your van I clicked off a few shots in case the tyre tracks tell us something we don't know."

"Maybe," she says, noncommittally. "Or maybe he flew in on a unicorn."

"You think it's a he?"

"I don't know. Maybe someone from the night Dad was killed." She swallows a yawn. "Sorry, big couple of days."

"You're out on your feet. Let me take you home and tuck you up in bed."

"I hope that's a proposition I can take a raincheck on. I want to sleep for a week."

"Like I said, I've got to go to work. The place is yours to do what you want. To be honest, knowing you're curled up in my bed waiting for my return is not a bad way to send a man off to work." He smiles over at her. "It'll make me rush home after shift."

"In your dreams."

"Most definitely. Preferably naked."

As Karin sinks into sleep, with the air conditioning blasting and dog curled up at her feet, her last thought is that if Lukah came home right now there would be no room for him in his own bed, and that would be the biggest pity of all.

Chapter 28

KARIN is brought from the depths of sleep with the phone vibrating beside her head.

She groans and rolls over, pulling the doona over her head, but the noise persists. She thinks it is a train going past but the sound is closer.

She reaches out a hand. "Hello."

"Nev Schultz is dead." Lukah's tone is urgent. "Get dressed and keep the dog with you till I get there."

Karin holds the phone in her hands after Lukah cuts the connection. Trouble has crept up the bed and his head rests in her lap as she sits staring into the dark.

Nev dead?

The fog in her brain begins to lift as the enormity of what Lukah told her sets in. The fact that he is rushing home says as much as the news itself. Nev's death isn't an accident. Just like the ransacking of her canvas wasn't an accident.

Someone is tidying up loose ends.

And Lukah is worried she is one of those loose ends.

She swings her legs over the edge of the bed and Trouble jumps to the floor, pressing close to her side.

She scratches his ears. "It's okay," she said softly. "The cavalry is coming."

Even so, she isn't sure whether to turn on every light in the house or to hide in the wardrobe. How did danger come at a person in towns like this? And what makes Lukah think that anyone knows she is staying with him?

There are too many questions.

She flicks on the lights and pulls on a pair of jeans and a T-shirt. And look back at the bed. So much for erotic dreams and Lukah's promise of a long slow wake-up. His phone call has put everything on hold, including any romantic ideas between the two of them.

As she moves through the house she switches on lights. Trouble, sensing something is wrong, stays close to her side. He must be desperate for a wee, but she isn't game to open the door and let him out.

How far away is Lukah?

Had he been at the police station when the news had come through about Nev, or had he been out somewhere. A car turns into the driveway with the screech and Karin sighs in relief. Someone coming to murder her wouldn't announce themselves with high beams and screeching tires, surely?

Next, she hears a key in the lock and the front door flings open. She stands in the shadows. Only when she is sure it is Lukah, she steps forward into his arms and clings to him while Trouble takes the opportunity to head outside and do his business.

"You're wearing more clothes than I'd hoped."

His effort to make her smile fails. "What happened?"

"The blokes down at the signal station called the station around seven o'clock. They told me there was a mess that I needed to deal with."

"A mess?" Karin covers her face.

Lukah gently removes her hands and pulls her back into his arms. "Trust me. You don't want to know."

"Not another train accident?"

Lukah shakes his head and pulls away. He calls the dog and waits while Trouble comes back and shuts the door. Then he takes her hand. "Come on into the kitchen. I could do with a cup of tea."

But it is he who puts the kettle on and busies himself with teabags and milk. Karin drops onto a chair with her elbows on the Laminex table, her fists clenching under her chin.

She watches him silently while he makes the tea and places a mug in front of her. He sits opposite and holds his cup in his hands.

"What's happening, Lukah? This can't all be because I came back for Jess's wedding."

Absently, he tips a spoonful of sugar into his tea and the last bit of milk from the carton. "It looks like an accident. The boys were working on one of the trucks. Changing a tyre. And the Jack gave way while Nev was underneath."

Karin gasps. "Nev was underneath?"

The trucks Lukah is talking about are huge, and the equipment needed to work on them specialised. But Nev has been around the trucks forever. He would be aware of the dangers.

"The men on his shift, did they say anything?"

Lukah shakes his head. "They were the change-over crew, fresh up from Perth. And Nev was in charge. I don't know why he was underneath the truck. That's usually one of the boys' jobs. My guess is something had gone wrong, and he was sorting it out. The poor bastards who found him didn't know what which way to look when they were telling me."

"And there was nobody else around?"

"The workshop is in a secure area. No unauthorized workers in or out without signing at the office."

"If it's where Trouble and I were the other day there was no way we could get through the barbed wire and "Keep Out" signs and not be noticed."

"Maybe it was an inside job." Lukah's gaze is somber.

Karin takes a sip of her tea. "You don't think it was an accident?"

"I'm not sure. There's been a lot of talk since you've been back. I probably should have told you before now."

Karin's gaze narrows. "What are they saying, exactly?"

"There's talk that you're here because you want revenge for your father's death."

"Revenge? I was sixteen."

"People have long memories. They remember your family. Some didn't like how your father was treated. How he lost his family's cattle station. They say he was screwed over by the brass just like they were."

"There can't be that many people left who would remember him," Karin says doubtfully. "Dad would be close to eighty if he was still alive and Nev is well into his seventies. I've already tried accessing the mine's files, but I didn't have any luck." She jumps to her feet. "Wait here. I've got an idea." She strides out of the room and returns with her laptop. She places it on the table and opens it. "Nev's files. Maybe there's something we missed."

"I thought the USB was stolen?"

"You think I'm an amateur." She grins across at him, relieved to be doing something, anything, to take her mind of the image of the dead man who was the one remaining link to her father. "I copied over all the files and encrypted them. Even if they had stolen my laptop—which they didn't—I would still have access to the files in the cloud."

She starts scrolling through the files while Lukah watches. She doesn't know why Nev saved all this stuff, but she is starting to get an inkling. She stops at a file marked, "Personnel, 2007" and opens it.

"That's the time they started talking about automation. From what I've read there was a lot of agitation, and it was directed at Dad because he was the one in charge of making the automation work. Some of the blokes thought he was doing them out of their jobs, and they got pretty vocal about it at the time."

"And here I was thinking you were lazing around the pool at the Tourist Park all day."

"Nah." She grins at him. "I was working." She brings up the file she was looking for and turns the laptop to face Lukah. "Any of these names familiar to you?"

He scans the list. And shakes his head. "None that I know. But I wasn't around back then. I was posted here in 2014."

"Lucky for you I have a second option." She swings the laptop back to her and scrolls through the files till she finds the one she is looking for.

"Goss?"

"Town gossip. I took another trip to the library and read through all the old newsletters. I knew they'd come in handy." She scrolls through the entries back to 2007 and slows. "What was the date of the first meeting to discuss the auto haul?"

He frowns. "The board meeting was in June. But it didn't go to vote until September."

"That's a start." She brings up the weekly newsletters for June. "Recognise any of these men?"

Lukah moves around the table to look over her shoulder as she begins slowly scrolling through image after image. "It was quite a big celebration when the automation kicked in," she said. "Big enough to bring a Senator to town."

Lukah points to one of the photos. "And a shipping magnate."

Karin continues to scroll through the images. There are several photos of Roland Maskell, Holden Caddel and Senator Brandon Flint together and separately.

Lukah studies the screen. "Follow the money?"

"No," Karin says softly. "Follow the power."

It's what Nev had been trying to tell her. That she was looking in the wrong place. Whether or not someone had taken it into their own hands and meted out justice by killing her father, the real crime had happened years ago. "But he never said anything."

"He knew he'd be wasting his time. It's amazing how people close ranks when it comes to self-interest. Even if Nev had spoken out no one would have listened to the crazy old coot. Sorry, but that's what everyone thought of Nev."

Karin isn't listening. She zooms in on an image. "Look at this photo. Roland and Julia Maskell, and the Senator and Rose."

Lukah bends to take a closer look. "I can't see anything."

"Maybe it's a woman thing. When I was talking to Mum about Rose. She said something that I didn't understand at the time."

"What was that?"

"She said the women were as much in love with Rose as the men were. What if it wasn't love in Julia's case? What if it was jealousy."

"Why would Julia Maskell be jealous of Rose? She had, and still has, everything money can buy."

"You'd think so, but Rose had the one thing Julia could never have. A baby."

"And you think after Rose died Julia Maskell kept the baby as her own. That's a big leap."

"It's the only thing that makes sense. Look at the photo of Julia and Rose, taken with my mother. Now look at the one taken last year of Julia and Jess. Don't you see? Julia isn't Jess's biological mother. Rose is."

Lukah stares at the photos. "We need evidence. DNA tests." His gaze his wary as he turns to her, warning. "Before we start jumping to conclusions."

Karin's fingers still on the keyboard. "When we were out at the station's cemetery, did you notice Rose's grave was up the back? Hidden. My father was silenced because he used Jess's parentage as leverage to protect his auto-haul technology. And now Nev is dead because he talked to me about what happened back then. I think my mother knows, too. I think it's why her friendship with Julia ended, and we moved to the city."

"If Jess's biological mother is Rose Caddel, then that makes her the Senator's daughter, not Roland Maskell's."

The enormity of Lukah's statement sits between them like an undetonated firework. Karin cannot imagine the effect of it going off. All the people burned. Lives destroyed. In a way, she almost wishes the truth didn't have to come out. For Jess's sake. But it is already out and there is no way to protect Jess from the reality that the life she has known all her life is about to come undone. But she has Grayson now, and Karin has to believe it is enough. Because there is no going back. Not after Nev. Not with what Karin now knows. She can't not right the wrongs of the past.

Exonerating her father will go a long way to healing the gut-wrenching pain she buried deep inside her the moment she learned he was never coming home again. She prays it will not come at the expense of her friend's happiness.

"What's totally crazy is that Julia believes her own fantasy, that Jess belongs to her. She kept it secret all these years. Until Jess asked for her birth certificate so she could marry Grayson. Julia knows there is no way she can hide the truth anymore. At least not from Jess."

"Unless Jess decided not to get married and elope instead."

With a sigh she shuts the laptop. "It was probably Julia's suggestion for all we know." She picks up her tea but makes no effort to drink it. "There's something else."

Lukah drops into the chair beside her. "There's more?"

She places the cup back down on the table, and it takes all her courage to turn and meet his gaze. "I think it was Julia Maskell who killed my father."

Chapter 29

"DAD knew about the baby. And, yes, he was probably blackmailing them to keep his hand in the game with the auto-haul technology. He didn't have access to the same capital that they did. And he had already gambled away Mulga Plains. He was probably desperate by the time he came up with the blackmailing idea. I think deep down, my father was a good man."

Lukah sits back in his chair. "Were we on the wrong track all this time? That this whole thing has never been about you uncovering corporate secrets. That it was personal."

"It's both. There's still a story, and it's big. But whether it's my story to write, I'm not so sure. My father was locked out of Damascus Holdings by his friends, probably because of the blackmail. I'm just not sure they knew how desperate Julia Maskell was to keep up the pretense that Jess belonged to her. And now the technology license is up for renewal, and they need to raise capital for the next stage. That's why they're all here."

"It was Jess's father who chose the wedding date. Jess told me that. And he's the one who has organised for Grayson and Jess to go to America for their honeymoon so Grayson can sign off on the paperwork over there."

Karin reopens the laptop. "A newsletter item from September 2009. At a gala event in June of that year there was an announcement about the technology. Look. Then, in September the technology is suddenly owned by new company. My father is no longer mentioned. I'm guessing that's when he threatened to go public with what he knew about the Senator's baby if they didn't include him in their deal. At some stage he must have confided in Uncle Bernie, who was still angry about Dad losing Mulga Plains. Uncle Bernie has stayed quiet all these years. Just in case."

"Let me guess. Protecting you is his just in case."

"I think so."

"But why get Nev to do his dirty work? Why didn't he tell you himself?"

"Mum," Karin says simply. "He protected her back in the day and he's still looking out for her now. He couldn't risk coming forward. Nev was the next best thing."

"Until it got him killed."

Car headlights swing into the driveway, interrupting them, and Lukah moves to the door. "It looks like we have a visitor."

Karin smiles grimly. "I thought we might."

"That was your uncle on the phone, wasn't it?"

Karin nods. "I knew he was around here somewhere. He had to be. Nev had the photo, and he gave it to me. I told Mum. I assumed Uncle Bernie knew about it, too."

Lukah stands in front of Karin and opens the door. "Stop right there."

Bernie held up his hands. "I come in peace. As soon as I heard about Nev Schultz I was on the next plane."

"You heard about the accident? In Perth? Bad news sure travels fast."

"I was hoping it wouldn't come to that."

"But you knew it might?"

"I knew certain people would stop at nothing to make sure the truth didn't get out." He looks at Lukah. "And might I suggest having this conversation on the street isn't not wise."

Lukah takes Karin's hand and ushers her into the kitchen, leaving Bernie to follow.

"Uncle Bernie, it's okay. We know about the blackmailing."

Bernie is about to reply when another car pulls. Doors slam and there are footsteps heading up the driveway. Fast.

"Why is the whole world up at the crack of dawn all of a sudden," Karin mutters as Lukah goes to open the front door.

She watched helplessly as Bec piles through the doorway, followed closely by Arno and Toby.

"What is this? A breakfast meeting?" Bec marches into the centre of the room and looks Karin's uncle up and down before turning back to Karin with one eyebrow raised. "Another senator?"

"My Uncle Bernie," Karin says. "He's here because of old Nev's accident."

"We heard about that," Bec replies. "It's why we're here."

"I tried to keep her home until a decent hour." Arno shrugs. "But it was like trying to hold back a volcano."

"Toby has something to tell you," Bec says to Lukah. "When he wakes up, that is."

Karin looks around at the group gathered around Lukah's kitchen bench. How has it come to this? Old Nev dead, her uncle flying up from the city in some kind of emergency dash, Bec and Arno racing over as soon as they heard the news. Jess and Grayson are God knows where.

It's Lukah who takes control. "Bec, we need to find Jess and Grayson as a matter of urgency. Any ideas?"

"What makes you think I know I know anything?"

"You wouldn't have dragged Toby out of bed at the crack of dawn if a) you weren't worried, or b) you didn't know something you think I should know."

Bec turns to Karin. "If you spent more time staying still and listening instead of racing all over the countryside, you would know, too."

Karin's gaze narrows on her friend. "Meaning?"

"When you guys took off to the coast, we spent the day around the pool." She shoots a smug look at Arno before continuing. "Arno and I may have snuck off for a bit, but Toby stayed poolside with your dog."

"Nobody pays attention to the youth of today." A new voice joins the conversation. Toby snakes an arm around his mother's waist and looks at Lukah. "I heard something important. Something my darling mother thinks is important enough to drag me over here at sparrow-fart."

"And what might that something be?" Lukah asks, suppressing a smile as Bec headlocks her son.

"What my foul-mouthed son means to say is he kindly agreed to join us this morning for fear of missing out on something exciting happening in his otherwise mundane screen-addled life."

Toby ducks out from his mother's arm and makes a beeline for the fridge. "The old bat told Jess and Grays to elope."

"You heard that?" Lukah looks at him sharply.

"I'm sixteen, not five. Duh!" He helps himself to a can of Coke, opens it and holds it up to his mother in salutation before taking a slurp.

Lukah's mouth tips into a smile. "And what did Jess say to that?"

"She said something about a birth certificate. But the oldie wouldn't give it to her. Then Jess was yelling something about a flower." At the sound of Toby's voice, Trouble barrels into the room. Toby drops the coke and grabs the dog. "A rose I think." he calls over his shoulder as the duo disappear into Lukah's study.

Karin's voice is sharp. "Did she say Damascus Rose, by any chance?"

"Yep, that's it," Toby replies. "Weird. Really weird." The door slams, leaving the adults looking at each other.

Lukah turns to Bec. "Do you know where they are now?"

"We think they may have taken the chopper to Karijini." Bec looks to Arno for confirmation. "And there's something else. Julia Maskell may have gone with them."

Lukah stares at her. "Are you sure?"

"No, but when we rang Windelema to see if Jess and Grayson arrived home safely, Roland Maskell answered the phone. He said that not only were Jess and Grayson not home, but his wife was gone, too. He said they were out at the Eco Retreat— and this is the weird part—that we needed to hurry if we wanted to stop them."

Arno slips an arm around Bec's shoulder and pulls her close, taking up the story. "We tried all their phone numbers last night, and again at first light, but none of them are answering. We were pondering what to do, when we remembered we had a policeman friend who could help us."

"So here we are." Bec's tone is even, but the worry in her eyes as she shoots a glance at Karin tells another story.

Lukah is about to reply when he his phone rings. "It's Grayson," he mouths, and hits speaker phone. "Hey, Grayson. We're all in my kitchen, deciding whether to get a posse together to come find you guys."

"Jess is gone." Grayson's voice is panicked. "I've looked everywhere."

"Start at the beginning," Lukah orders, holding up a hand for everyone to be quiet.

"We were going to get married without all the fuss." The stress in Grayson's voice is palpable. "Julia is here with us. She organised a celebrant and wanted to be with us when we exchanged our vows. First thing this morning, she knocked on our door to take Jess to see the sunrise. She said it was a mother and daughter thing. But they haven't returned."

Karin shoots Lukah a frantic look. "We need to get out there," she mouths.

Lukah nods and takes the call off speaker. He talks urgently into the phone and points towards his car keys. Karin snatches then up and heads for the front door, Lukah hard on her heels.

"We're coming, too." Bec drags Arno's after them.

"I'll stay with the boy," Uncle Bernie promises. "And the dog. You can't take a dog into a National Park."

Karin hesitates. She isn't sure of Uncle Bernie's role in all this. But he isn't a killer. She looks towards Bec who nods.

Lukah takes the keys from Karin and hustles them out to the car. "Let's go."

The sun is rising in the sky along with the heat as Lukah pulls into the Eco Retreat. Grayson is pacing up and down out the front.

"Where's Jess?

"They were heading to the lookout." Grayson points to a track that leads to the Joffre Gorge. "But they should have been back long before now. Unless they decided to climb down for a swim."

"Julia is not Jess's mother," Karin says shortly. "And I think Jess may have worked it out."

Grayson pales. "Julia suggested the lookout for the ceremony. She said it would be romantic."

Karin doesn't wait to hear anymore. She turns and starts to run, Lukah close at her heels. "Which way?" she says wildly.

"Follow me." Lukah takes the lead. As part of his rescue training, he knows his way around better than she does. And right now, they need every second they can get. As they run, Karin hears Grayson and Arno's footsteps behind them. Bec stays at the retreat and calls for backup.

Luke comes to a halt at the Lookout sign. "They'll be out there. We don't want to startle them." He slows to a walk and takes Karin's hand. "Follow my lead."

Julia and Jess are where Lukah says they'll be. Julia is standing beside Jess, their backs to the gorge.

Julia looks up as they approach. "Good morning. Have you come to see the happy couple exchange vows." She turns to her daughter. "It will be nice to have your friends as witnesses, won't it, darling."

Jess signals to Karin with her eyes as she nods at her mother's words. *Be careful.*

Karin understands. "That's why we're here, Mrs Maskell. I'm glad we made it in time. Is there anything we can do to help you set up?"

Julia smiles but her there is a glint in her eyes that makes Karin shiver. "There's so much to do. I thought the children eloping would make it so much easier, but that was before."

Karin takes a cautious step forward. "Before?"

"The guests are starting to arrive at the station for the wedding," Julia replies. "And this naughty girl decides to run off, causing all sorts of distress." Julia's grip is tight on Jess's arm. "I came to talk some sense into her."

"I'm here to help now," Karin replies, keeping her gaze locked on Julia's. "Bridesmaid's duties. How about we head back to the retreat for breakfast and decide what to do next."

"The marriage celebrant will be here any minute." Julia's voice rises an octave. "I brought the dress with me. Jess, you're not dressed. Why aren't you dressed?"

Karin meets Jess's gaze above her mother's head. Karin isn't sure about this part of the story.

"Mother organised for us to get married out here without all the fuss," Jess's voice is shaking, her gaze locked on Karin. "Imagine our delight when she decided to fly in for the ceremony. You're right, Mumsie. I need to change into my beautiful dress—"

"Your father should be here," Julie continues as if Jess hasn't spoken. "It's only right." She drags Jess closer to the edge, turning to look down at the gorge. "I invited him, you know."

Karin swallows. "The Senator said he'll be here. But he's running late. Do you think we can hold off the ceremony for a couple of hours?"

"It needs to be now," Julia snaps, then her voice calms. "You don't understand. Roland has organised for Demascus Holdings to meet this afternoon. And Jess and Grayson need to be married by then. Or Jess won't be part of it. Only Grayson. And that wouldn't be fair. Her mother—I'm mean Damascus Rose would have wanted Jess to inherit her fortune, not those men. They plan to sell it out from under her. Damascus Holdings will be nothing but a shell company by the time they're finished. They don't think I know, but I do. And I'm going to stop them. For my baby. For you, Jess. And for Rose."

"Is that why you organised for Jess and Grayson to be married this morning?" Karin's voice is soft. "To protect Jess's interests when the Directors vote to move the assets."

Julia nods. "Yes," she says, her eyes glazing." I didn't want Jess to end up like me. I didn't want them to sign away her future. I wanted to protect her. I'm doing this for you, Jess. For my daughter."

"I am your daughter," Jess says quietly. "You know that. Rose may have been my birth mother, but she's not with us anymore. You raised me. I'm your daughter and you're my mother in every way that matters."

"Except on your birth certificate," Julia replies, her voice cracking. "Everyone will know you're hers. Roland says we can't let the secret get out. Too many people have too much to lose, he says. I'm sorry, my darling. I tried to make it right. I tried so hard—"

And before anyone can move, Julia's grip loosens on Jess's arm, and it is Jess's turn to throw her arms around her mother, trying to haul her away from the edge. But Julia is strong, fueled by too many years of pain and betrayal and keeping a secret too enormous for her to hold inside. And not the secret is out, it is replaced with rage, a rage so strong it is propelling them both inexorably towards the edge of the precipice.

"No—" Karin starts forward, but Lukah holds her back.

"Wait," he orders curtly. Karin feels herself being pushed behind him as he strides forward. "Don't move."

The authority it in his voice is enough for Julia to freeze momentarily, and in that moment, Lukah lunges, knocking both women sideways. With Jess free, he holds Julia down with his body.

Karin runs and drags her friend into her arms. "It's okay. It's over now."

But it isn't.

As Karin turns and Lukah raises himself from the ground, Julia lunges, and propels herself over the cliff. *"Jessalynnnn."* Her guttural cry echoes across the stillness.

A strangled cry rips from Jess's throat. "Noooo!" And she burrows her head into the strength of Karin's embrace.

Julia's screams fade. And the gorge is silent except for the cry of a lone corella as it flies after its flock.

"I'm sorry, Jess." Karin holds the shaking woman in her arms. "I'm so sorry."

And then Grayson is there, peeling Jess out of Karin's arms and scooping her up in his arms. "I'm taking her back the Retreat." He looks over at Lukah. "Are you okay to handle things here."

Lukah nods as he stares down into the gorge. "Karin, go with them."

"No," she says quietly. "I'm waiting here. With you."

After Grayson carries his sobbing fiancée away, Lukah and Arno begin the descent down the gorge while Karin waits for the Emergency Services. Even though there is only one outcome for this tragedy, they need to retrieve the body of the poor crazed woman who felt she had no other out.

And in some dark place in her heart, Karin understands. *The sins of our fathers come to rest on the children. As do the sins of our mothers.*

Chapter 30

T HE pre-dawn rays light up the mountain as Karin lines up white plastic chairs in neat rows. Lukah and Arno are setting up gazebos while Bec takes care of the bride.

It's an impromptu affair and everyone has a job to do including Toby and the dog who walk the perimeter of J & J Constructions, making sure the chain wire fencing is secure, and the current mouse plague is under control. If they get distracted every now and again collecting rocks, then that's okay with the adults.

Bec has been allocated the job of getting Jess ready at the house while Grayson is in shorts and T-shirt helping with the setup, his penguin suit hanging in Jess's office. They have an hour.

The sun will hit the mountain at 6:32 am, the planned time for Jess and Grayson's nuptials. Bec and Karin have raided the local gardens for frangipani, bougainvillea and anything else with a bit of colour, and Karin is currently sprinkling the petals over white linen tablecloths pilfered from the catering shed at the mine-site.

Jess's construction yards have been cleared of heavy machinery courtesy of her team who have all been promised a seat at the wedding and are currently at home rounding up wives and children and anything that resembles suits and bowties, even though the hastily texted invitations make it clear the suits aren't necessary. But any event is an excuse for dressing up out here and no one is going to miss the opportunity of attending Jess's wedding in anything but their best.

In front of a chain wire mesh fence the three-piece orchestra is tuning up while site workers make short work of dismantling the fencing around them. Like it is every day they perform under such conditions, the orchestra happily tune their instruments and chat to the workers, promising to play each man's favourite tune.

It may not be the spectacular Karijini gorges the Pilbara is renowned for, but Mt Nameless in the pre-dawn light comes close.

The mountain.

Where it all started and hopefully where it will end.

New beginnings.

Karin and Bec had put their heads together at the Eco-Lodge and come up with a new plan. Jess had shaken her head while Bec cracked up with laughter. Jess was used to crews and big trucks at her workplace. The idea of clearing the place out and turning it into a wedding venue is so ludicrous she can only nod in agreement at her bridesmaid's crazy plan.

The three women hold hands and plan and try not to think of Lukah and Arno down the gorge on a rescue mission that is already too late.

The women talk of other things.

Of futures.

And slowly Jess's hand stops trembling as it rests on Grayson's knee.

Her fiancé, who is never far from her side, only agrees to let his bride out of his sight this morning so that Bec can whisk her away to work her magic on the traumatised bride-to-be. Then proceeds to text every ten minutes for a welfare check. Hence, the groom is little help with the wedding set-up as he monitors his phone instead of pitching gazebos and stringing up decorations.

Lukah reverses trucks out onto the street and removes diggers and every other piece of machinery with a key in it from the site. While Karin herds a group of wives busily slamming shut shed doors and stringing metres of hastily gathered linen over trestle tables their spouses had set up.

And there are more beer Eskies than Karin can count, some worse for wear from one too many fishing trips, but stocked and ready to quench the thirst of the early morning revelers.

When a community comes together it sure comes together. Karin watches as Ray's bakery truck pulls up at the wide-open gates accommodating everyone's coming and going. After an all-night baking session, Ray is delivering not only his legendary meat pies, but also platters of savouries, cheeses and fruits, along with a dozen cases of Veuve Clicquot. Her hastily texted request had been for a coffee machine and croissants. She should have known better.

And if they raided the supermarket freezers for fresh strawberries and watermelon and rock melon, and whatever other fruits they could find, who is she to argue?

She eyes the barbecue set up in front of one of the sheds. One of Jess's workers is happily flipping eggs and turning bacon, and a queue is already forming, as weary workers attracted by the aroma of food, take a break. Most of them are still in T-shirts and shorts, with instructions to change into suits when they are done.

This wedding is going to do the town proud. Organised and pulled together during an all-night session by Bec and her team of friends. While Grayson and Jess slept, guarded by Toby and Trouble who set up camp in the hallway of Lukah's house. Bernie is master of ceremonies and celebrant rolled into one.

Karin sets up the bridal table and is surveying her handiwork as Lukah comes and stands behind her.

"Not a bad effort," he says, wrapping his arms around her waist.

Karin leans back against him. "Not bad, except nobody has had any sleep, except for the bride and groom."

"Don't worry, these guys are used to working all night and then knocking back a few beers before they kip. If you're worried about them going the distance, Bernie may have pulled a few strings over at the mine and organised shift swaps so they guys can enjoy the wedding and sleep off the celebrations without worrying about waking up for work."

"And the police? They're going to stand guard and make sure this wedding goes off without a hitch?"

"If you're asking about Roland Maskell or the Senator turning up, then you don't need to worry on that account either. There will be no gatecrashing of the wedding by anyone who has not been invited. But just in case, Bernie has organised a security contingent from the mine, and they will be on the gate for the morning. Nobody in or out without being on the list. And Bec's list is impressive. Stop worrying."

Karin summons a smile. "You forgot to mention perimeter patrol."

Toby has placed a bowtie around Trouble's collar and his leash is covered in black velvet to match the velvet of Toby's vest. Toby has agreed to wear a button-down shirt because it is a special occasion, but he is sporting his favourite *Son Brother Gamer Legend* T-shirt underneath.

An air-horn sounds. Lukah drops his arms from around Karin's waist and spins her around to drop a quick kiss on her nose. "No rest for the wicked. I'll see you at the ceremony."

Karin looks to where the horn had blasted and sees a row of ablutions on the back of a semi-trailer. Lukah is already organizing willing hands to unload and set up the toilets around the back of Jess's work sheds.

The sun is starting to make its presence felt.

Right on time Karin hears the blast of a car's horn getting louder as it approaches, signaling the arrival of the bride. She smooths the satin of her strapless maroon dress, collects her posy of wildflowers strung together with raffia from the Esky, and makes her way to the gates of the worksite.

Everyone scrambles to take up their positions.

The groom and groomsmen move to where Bernie has set up an arch with a ceremony table covered in white linen. Grayson stands under the arch with his back to the mountain, impeccably dressed in a black tuxedo and bowtie. His eyes trained on the arrival of his bride. Beside him Lukah and Arno do their best not to pull at the necks of the shirts. They are grinning like fools as they look from Grayson to where Karin is opening the back door of the car.

Bec alights in a strapless dress in the same shade of maroon as the one Karin is wearing, followed by Jess in simple white sheath that clings to her body and falls away to the ground.

Karin and Bec move to take up their positions in front of Jess as the orchestra plays the opening chords of "Here Comes the Bride", but they are too late. Jess looks around, oblivious to what has happened to her workspace, and spots Grayson. There is no slow walk down the aisle, merely a hitching of her dress as she strides towards him.

Bec groans. "Satin and work boots. Just the way we planned it."

Karin laughs. "Something tells me Grayson isn't looking at her feet."

They watch as Jess flings herself into Grayson's arms and kisses him soundly.

Bec crooks her arm. "Shall we?"

Karin grins and slips her arm through her friend's. "Don't mind if I do."

They walk sedately behind Jess, with Karin holding firmly to Bec's arm lest she stop and chat to her friends on the way through. They arrive the ceremony table and line up opposite the groomsmen.

Bernie nods at the orchestra and holds up a hand. "Listen up, you pair," he orders the bride and groom. "I've got a job to do and that means no more snogging until I make it legal."

The first rays of the sun hit the mountain as Jess and Grayson exchanged vows. Their guests whoop and cheer and stomp their feet in the dust while the orchestra keeps up with aplomb. In the middle of the melee Trouble runs out-of-control circles around the bridal party with Toby in hot pursuit. While Bec holds her hands up to her face and groans at the destruction of her perfect wedding plans. A waiter places a glass of champagne in her hand.

Under Ray's careful supervision everyone is given champagne or beer, and the salutations begin in earnest.

It is romantic and crazy and a wedding none of them will forget.

The bridal party settle to the table Karin decorated, and guests pick up plastic chairs and move at will between platters and beer Eskies.

Amid the chaos, Jess turns to her friends. "I don't know how you did it, but it's perfect."

"That's what friends are for." Bec raises her champagne glass. "I think." She leans against Arno who catches the glass. She leans into him. "Remind me to never get married. It's too much work."

If Karin isn't mistaken, Bec has just hit her wall.

Karin takes a sip her champagne and places it back on the table. Like Bec, she hasn't slept. Or eaten, come to think of it. Just as her empty stomach gives an inelegant grumble, Ray appears in front of her with a silver platter. Neat rows of circular fruit; rockmelon, pineapple and watermelon drizzled with strawberries and grapes and blueberries.

"How—"

He drops an eye in a discreet wink. "Your boyfriend is not the only one who can fly a plane."

"Do you have a license?"

"It was an emergency. Besides, we needed to collect something from Karratha and you lot were busy."

Karin's mouth drops as he nods in the direction of the catering truck. Wheeling towards them on a trolley pushed by two girls in neat waitress outfits, is the biggest cake Karin has ever seen.

A bride and groom in mining outfits stand hand in hand at the top of the cake.

Karin feels tears begin to well, whether from exhaustion or emotion she isn't sure, but before she can speak, Ray holds up his hand.

"It's what we do," he says softly. "Pulling together in good times and bad. This is one of the good times. So, no tears, okay?"

He's right. Karin thanks him with a watery smile.

Lukah stands, picks up the knife and passes it to Jess. "It's tradition that the bride cuts the cake."

Jess takes it with trembling hands and stands.

She drives the knife into the cake. "Thank you all for celebrating with us." She looks around her construction site. "My office and yards have never looked so neat. Or clean." She smiles down at Bec who is leaning against Arno's shoulder, her mouth slightly open and, if Karin isn't mistaken, gently snoring.

"And I'm assuming someone will tell me later were all my equipment's gone." There is laughter and one comment about how they'll think about it while she is away on her honeymoon. "A week," she says. "We close up shop for a week. Then it's back to work for everyone."

There is a general cheer at her words. "But for now I want to thank my friends for this beautiful setting and the most perfect wedding a girl could ask for."

Jess sobers as she raises her glass. "There's one more person I want to thank. She's not here with us but without her today would not have been possible. To my mother, Julia Maskell. To all of you celebrating with me and Grayson today, my mother taught me that one thing matters more than anything in this world. Family. There's an old say that money is root of all evil. In my family's case that may have turned out to be true. But without everything that has happened in my life, I would never have met the man of my dreams."

She pauses and looks down at her husband, before returning her gaze to her friends. "Grayson and I have decided that we will keep J & J Constructions." She pats her stomach. "After Junior is born—"

It is impossible for her to continue over the cheers. She admits defeat with a shrug and pulls her husband to his feet and proceeds to kiss him soundly while the laughter and cheers continue around them.

"—but I also know that you're all here to help," she says once order is restored. "That you are my family and always will be."

Jess is right, Karin realises through her tears. Regardless of what her parents have done, Jess and Grayson will make things right. And one day their children will hear their story with pride, not sadness.

"Finally, I'd like to propose a toast to my beautiful bridesmaids, Karin and Rebecca. Friends forever."

Karin swipes her hand across her eyes and looks up at the mountain. It seems forever ago that she had climbed it with Jess and Bec. When she had told them about Damascus Rose. So much heartbreak caused by the secrets and lies of others. Julia Maskell had kept a secret so big it had finally destroyed her.

Jess will be okay, but she will not forget or easily forgive the men who caused so much grief. Karin turns her back to the mountain and looks around at the people surrounding the newly married couple.

And in that moment, she knows old Nev is wrong. It isn't money and power that matters. It's people; family and friends and community.

She turns to the man at her side and takes his hand. "Let's get out of here," she says softly. "I think the party can go on without the local police watching over it."

They slip out the chain-wire gates and nobody notices them leave. Jess is where she needs to be, surrounded by her friends, and Arno will take care of Toby until Bec wakes up and realises she's missing the party. As for Trouble, he is in doggie heaven with so much food being slipped his way. He will sleep for a week when the excitement is over.

She takes Lukah's hand, and they walk side by side in silence. Coming home has been cathartic. She has laid her ghosts to rest. There are no words for what is between her and Lukah. Only time will tell what the future holds.

Right now, being with him is enough.

Out next...

A POWERFUL ADVERSARY, a corrupt judicial system and a woman determined to reclaim what is rightfully hers.

In the heart of the unforgiving outback, Karin Baxter steps into the lion's den of PMB Pastoral, fully aware that her quest for justice might be her last. With a Royal Commission breathing down their necks, $400 million in daily exports, and the honor of one of Western Australia's most influential families on the line, the stakes couldn't be higher. Karin's only weapons are a crude map sketched on a beer coaster and the whispered tales from her father's knee. As she digs deeper into the secrets buried on her family's former land, she realizes that some will stop at nothing to keep the truth hidden. With powerful adversaries closing in and a corrupt judicial system stacked against her, Karin must navigate a treacherous path to reclaim her rightful inheritance. Will she survive the relentless pursuit of those determined to silence her, or will the weight of power and corruption crush her fight for justice? In this high-stakes thriller, the line between right and wrong blurs, and the cost of truth may be more than Karin is willing to pay.

Don't miss out!

Visit the website below and you can sign up to receive emails whenever Mel Hammond publishes a new book. There's no charge and no obligation.

https://books2read.com/r/B-A-KHLD-AHKFG

Connecting independent readers to independent writers.

Also by Mel Hammond

A Gillies Ridge Novella
Christmas Belles

Standalone
The Voices in Your Head: Story Writing Guidelines
TIPS: Advice From Bestselling Authors to Help You on Your Writing
Journey
Nameless

Watch for more at www.melhammond.com.au.

About the Author

Mel Hammond is and Australian romance author who travels the country in her van making up stories about strong capable heroines who can save themselves in any situation but it helps if a ruggedly handsome hero strides onto the page to lend a helping hand. Mel has always made a living from her writing, whether it be journalism, travel writing, podcasting, or teaching High School English. She has published literary and middle grade fiction, but her current obsessions are romantic comedies and small town coastal romances.

Read more at www.melhammond.com.au.